# THESE CHAI

CW00556716

## Michael Arlen

Michael Arlen was born in Bulga.                    _...ı parents,
changing his name from Dikran ..unyounmdjian in 1922 and
becoming a naturalised British subject. Educated at Malvern
College, he wrote two early novels which met with little attention.
He achieved fame with the publication of *The Green Hat* in 1924.
Driving around London in an enormous yellow Rolls Royce, slim,
well-dressed and impeccably mannered, he seemed not unlike the
characters in his novels. He lived in Cannes until the outbreak of
the Second World War, and then moved to New York where he died
in 1956.

**Emma Tennant** has established a worldwide reputation for
original fiction as well as novels based on the characters and
situations from well loved classics. Best known of the latter
category is *Pemberley*, a sequel to Jane Austen's *Pride and Prejudice*.

These Charming People

# These Charming People

Michael Arlen

FOREWORD BY EMMA TENNANT

CAPUCHIN CLASSICS

# CAPUCHIN CLASSICS
## LONDON

## These Charming People

First published 1923
This edition published by Capuchin Classics 2010

© Michael Arlen Jnr 1923
2 4 6 8 0 9 7 5 3 1

Capuchin Classics
128 Kensington Church Street, London W8 4BH
Telephone: +44 (0)20 7221 7166
Fax: +44 (0)20 7792 9288
E-mail: info@capuchin-classics.co.uk
www.capuchin-classics.co.uk

*Châtelaine of Capuchin Classics*: Emma Howard

ISBN: 978-0-9562947-1-5

# Foreword

"Of all the company, only an intimate few stayed on at Malmanor after the Monday morning. Of the women, Mrs Loyalty, the Lady Fay Paradise, Esther Carlyle (who kept house for her brother), Mrs Avalon, and Shelmerdene. Of the men, Ralph Loyalty, George Tarlyon, John Avalon, myself, our host, and young Raymond Paris, the novelist, who spent his mornings in a secluded room, writing …"

This opening to the first story in *These Charming People* had an instant effect on me. At first, as I looked through the small collection, saw that the nightingale singing in Berkeley Square had come from him – along with the fancy names of Arlen's cast of characters and the geographical strictures imposed by his limiting of the action to Mayfair – I found myself recognising a world I had never known; the between-wars of the 1920s. Here was my Aunt Clare, who had married three times and divorced an equal number of *decree nisis* until her fabled beauty disappeared and she was left only with a rejection slip from her last admirer, known as "the General" stating "let's face it, we've had it". (Modern langage for its time.) And here were the houses with ball-rooms where she had danced the night through, probably accompanied by the nightingale. This was the world of Gosford Park, of valets and maids and spiteful chit-chat: I had sensed her loyalty to the outworn values represented (so I imagined) by the Tarlyons and the Avalons and the lovely Shelmerdene – and I had secretly thanked my lucky stars that the world my father and his siblings had been reared in had been removed by the second world war and could never return. I giggled – as who wouldn't – at the remoteness of the men as described by Arlen: like a jigsaw puzzle of Empire, they were representative of the vast possessions in the Colonies and could be slotted together all over the Globe, returning on occasion to their old haunts in Mayfair: Davies Street and Grosvenor Square and the nightingale's favourite haunt (as I imagined it) in the leafy trees of Berkeley Square. The hawk-nosed men fell in and out of love with white-throated women in flowing, diaphanous gowns – and then left them, to serve the ruling deity, Empire.

So far so good. But as I read on, through these extraordinary stories – *The Smell In the Library* where a practical joke guides the action, *The Hunter After Wild Beasts* ("Listen, Gloria," he whispered. "When I found you had gone, my life cracked like an earthenware cup… and now," he said, "you have mended it again.") I began to realise that the author of *The Green Hat*, the Armenian-born Michael Arlen, had succeeded in producing something quite unlike the melodrama that can be laughed at like an old movie. He was producing satire, yes, but a satire which transcended the normal rules of the game – for the tragic-comic effect he set down on the page delineated exactly an era of transformation. The strangled emotions of his hawk-nosed men, and the cool sarcasm expressed by his well-born heroines show the beginning of the end of Empire: Arlen is laughing along with us but he is also deadly serious.

Enjoy these stories for what they are – a record of a world escaping the nobility of sadness after the horrors of the First World War and heading for the 30s, the age of cynicism and anxiety. The beautiful Shelmerdene will laugh with you – but she is aware of the world she has entered – much more aware than my Aunt Clare.

*Emma Tennant*
*London, September 2009*

# CONTENTS

# Introducing a Lady of No Importance and a Gentleman of Even Less

There was, and (by the grace of God) there still is, a lovely woman whom it once pleased a young man to call Shelmerdene, because, he said, though it is not her real name, it becomes her better than any real name could. And about Shelmerdene books have been written and for her men have died, which just shows you the sort of woman she was. Now it happened one day that Shelmerdene returned to England after a long absence abroad in Persia, but I can tell you nothing about that because I know nothing of Persia, except that it is rather inadequately governed by a Shah who is a pretty fat young man and wears a diamond in his hat.

Among other entertainments that we, her friends, contrived for Shelmerdene, as a welcome and a token of our enduring affection, a great house-party was arranged by Aubrey Carlyle; whereby, on a week-end in May, a great company of agreeable people was gathered together at Malmanor Park, a vast Elizabethan sort of place in ancient red that lies on a velvet plain between a brooding hill and the peculiar wood of Carmion; for it is said of Carmion Wood that only foreigners may hear the singing of the birds therein, whereas for Englishmen there is nothing but the sighing of the boughs and the rustling of the leaves. What truth there is in that legend I do not know, but I don't suppose there is much.

Of all the company, only an intimate few stayed on at Malmanor after the Monday morning. Of the women, Mrs. Loyalty, the Lady Fay Paradise, Esther Carlyle (who kept house for her brother), Mrs. Avalon, and Shelmerdene. Of the men, Ralph Loyalty, George Tarlyon, John Avalon, myself, our host, and young Raymond Paris, the novelist, who spent his mornings in a secluded room writing.

One morning young Raymond Paris had sat long at the large table in his room—an upstairs room it was which Aubrey Carlyle had put at his disposal—but the paper before him was as white as a woman's throat; nor is the likeness too unfair, as are most likenesses of this sort, for Raymond Paris had an extravagant taste in foolscap, being still young enough to enjoy the actual writing of his tales as much as the fame and fortune they might in due course bring him. Established writers used to ask him: "What, don't you typewrite your stories straight away? Or don't you dictate them? Well, you'll soon get into the habit of it." And that used to depress young Raymond Paris, for he did not want to get into the habit of it, he liked seeing his thoughts making patterns on the white paper.

But this morning the white paper before him remained far too white for his liking. The table at which he sat with a worried face was drawn across the bow of the wide windows; and through them the eyes were enticed by a long avenue of tall trees, which swept massively away from the gardens for many furlongs and was at last joined to the border of Carmion Wood; but, nearer, the eyes dropped from the windows to the upper garden, where—for the month was May—lay many beds of rare tulips, the whole drawn to an exquisite though, perhaps, intemperate design. Pink and purple, red and yellow, white and magenta, the carnival of gay tall tulips flamed in the sunlight and swayed to the lilt of the gentle wind, so that the young man's brooding eyes likened them to glittering soldiers who every now and then stooped to the elegant distraction of a valse. . . .

"So this is the way you work, Raymond Paris!" cried a soft, light voice behind him, and never was a young man with his way to make in the world more grateful for being disturbed.

"I am in great trouble, Shelmerdene. For here have I been offered an untold sum for a short-story, and I have not the glimmer of an idea! The editor wrote to me saying that he wanted something not only witty but serious, something earnest as well as gay, and with a point. Now isn't that an unfair thing to ask of a man?" And the young writer looked up at Shelmerdene with a self-pitying smile, while she stood beside him, playing thoughtfully with the catch of an ancient pink shagreen cigarette-case, which had once been vanity-box in chief to Queen Marie Antoinette, so they said.

Now who shall describe Shelmerdene of the dark sleek hair, of the lips that smiled unaccountably, of the blue eyes that were gentle and witty and alight with understanding? She was lithe and dark-haired, and her face was white, and her eyes were as blue as night and as impersonal as the stars. She wore, this morning, a jumper of vermilion silk, and her skirt was thus and thus, and sweetly rakish on her head was a brown felt hat with a wide stiff brim, and on her feet were brown brogues of Russian leather, such as only men-servants can properly polish, women being what they are.

Shelmerdene smiled down at Raymond Paris, the young writer who could not write a story.

"I will tell you a story," she said. "I will tell it quite plainly, but afterwards you may decorate it with fine words and epigrams, and make it a story fit for an editor to read. No, I won't sit down, but you may continue to. This story, my dear, begins with me. All my stories do, though they generally end with some one else; that is called making a mess of one's life, Raymond. I was married very young, and an unhappy marriage it was, so that we parted rather grimly, that queer man and I. He would not divorce me and I could not divorce him, for he was a pure man. Somewhere in this world, Raymond, there is a stern man who is my husband, and you must always remember that in any conversation with me, for he is not at all the kind of man whom one can forget. I have tried to, and so I know. He was very good-looking in a naval sort of way—which was just as well, as he was in the navy—and his eyes had that bleary, bitten look which they tell you comes from being out on the high seas in all weathers, but you and I know that it comes from drinking gin-and-bitters at all hours, there being so little else to do on a battleship. Anyway, there he is and here am I; pride parted us once, and now the years part us, and God only knows what will happen, if indeed He's at all interested in such silly people.

"I fell in love. 'Fall' is exactly the word in this context, and I did not rise quickly. That is called being a loose woman, Raymond, but you need not put this part into your story; I am just explaining myself to you out of affection and because it is a May morning.

"My story is about how I fell in love with a stone image; for women are sometimes like sea-birds, they sometimes worship stone images, men who are carved of the rocky stuff of life. . . . All men and women are in a conspiracy to hide a secret, and the secret that lies in the hearts of all men and women is that they want to be loved. It sounds almost too pathetic, Raymond, but it is true. I fell in love with this young man, and I wanted to be loved by him. But he would not—Raymond, do you understand, he would not love me! Those, of course, were not his exact words, but it came to that. Why is it always the wrong men who fall in love with one, Raymond? My lovely stone image told me that he didn't deserve being loved by me, because, because—oh, how the poor boy hesitated!—he hadn't it in him to love any one. He simply couldn't love, he said— and he felt such a brute! And then he tried to weigh his words carefully. He liked me, he said, as much as he could like, but he didn't *think* he loved me—mark that glorious, arrogant *think*, Raymond! And also tell me when I am boring you. . . .

"As he spoke, over luncheon it was, I watched the blue eyes which tried to look straight into mine but couldn't, because he was shy. He was trying to be honest with me, you see, and trying to be honest with women makes men shy. He felt such a brute, he kept on saying, he . . . yes, he did love me in his way, he suddenly admitted. But his way wasn't, simply couldn't be, mine. He simply couldn't give himself wholly to any one—and he so frightfully wanted to, he felt he was missing such lovely things!

"I was a fool, of course—I mean, to believe what he said about not loving me. Oh, what an utter fool I was to believe him! But, all the same, I clung to my pathetic love-affair with both hands, ever so tight. I did indeed, Raymond. It is extraordinary how unattainable a woman can make a man she isn't sure of! Maybe you have been unattainable to some woman, Raymond, or maybe you will be. It will be fun for you.

"If it hadn't been that my husband would not divorce me I would have dragged that lovely stone-image to the altar. It would have been better so, our lives would have been quite different and perhaps quite beautiful; but what actually happened was also quite beautiful, in an irregular kind of way.

"I had set out, you see, to make myself essential to him, mentally, physically, every way. If he couldn't love me as a man loves a woman then he must love me as a tree loves the creepers that cling round it. Oh dear, how extraordinarily silly one gets! I was terribly serious, Raymond. I always am, which is perhaps what keeps me young—but do I look young, youngish? Quick, tell me! Oh, you are sweet, Raymond!

"But I hadn't much time in which to make myself necessary to him—that young man who said he couldn't give himself wholly to any woman, who sandwiched a woman between a dead salmon and a dead grouse! He was the eldest son of a great house, but in the meantime he was a soldier, and he had the frozen blue eyes which make a good soldier, as soldiers go—and he *was* going, Raymond! under special orders for East Africa, where he would have to stay several months. Just a few weeks I had, then, to make him feel that he couldn't bear life, in Africa or anywhere else, without me. And, my dear, the world didn't hold a more perfect dream than that in which he would come to me and offer to risk his career for me! That is what is called being a cad, Raymond, and women are rather good at it. I wanted him to offer me his ambition, and then I would consider whether or not I would give it back to him. But he didn't. I lost.

"And I had seemed so like winning, too! For, ten days before he was to sail, he had insisted on taking me away from London, saying that London was getting between us and that we must go away into the country, just to breathe and to love. That is not, of course, how he put it, Raymond, but that was his meaning, and very, very happy it made me. Imagine! Seven days we spent together in a funny sweet little inn under the shadows of those toy hills which are called mountains in Wales; but I will not tell you about those days, for they are a very intimate memory, and even if I did you could not put them into your story, for your editor would wonder if you were mad, saying that the British public will put up with much but not with as much as that. But, all the same, they were a wonderful seven days, and as we sat silently facing each other in the train back to London, silent because there was too much to talk about, I knew I had won. There were three days left.

"In London he dropped me at my house, and he was to return in the evening to take me out to dinner. But he was back within an hour, and when I went downstairs I found him pacing impatiently up and down the drawing-room. He told me that his orders had been changed; he had to go to Paris first, and then take ship at Marseilles.

'To Paris!' I said, not understanding.

"'Yes, to-night, in two hours,' he said quickly, shyly. He was embarrassed at the idea of a possible scene. And oh, those frozen blue eyes, those frozen blue eyes of pro-consular men! He must go at once, he said. He shook both my hands; and he held them a little while in that pathetic attempt at tenderness which sometimes overtakes Englishmen when they are eager to go and do something else. He would write to me, he said. He mumbled something about my being a darling, but I simply hadn't a word. It was all just as though nothing had ever happened to us, as though we had never been to the little Welsh inn, or played and laughed and loved, as though he had never begged me to run my fingers through his hair because I had said his hair was a garden where golden flowers grew. Englishmen are very odd, Raymond. He was going away! But he would write to me, he said, and would be back in twelve months or so . . . and he almost forgot to kiss me. But what are kisses?

"Now this is where, Raymond, in writing this story, your craftsmanship must come in. You must be very clever just here, Raymond. You must manage to convey that, though I was not a bad loser by nature, I was terribly wretched for a time: that I simply didn't exist. You must fill in the gap with some fine prose and acute observation—the horrible gap between the time he went away and the time when I again began to take notice of life. You can't both be loyal to me and true to life, Raymond, so you had better be romantic about it. You will find it quite easy to be romantic about other people's troubles.

"I didn't forget him. I have never forgotten him, that stone image which stood in my heart and then broke itself to pieces because of some law I did not, do not, understand. But there is a law I do understand, a cruel kind of law, and that is the law of reaction. He wrote me letters at long intervals; cold, honest bits of writing, strong-and-silent-backbone-of-Empire stuff, and rather pompous with their appreciations of me tacked on to descriptions of the desert and the natives. But I wrote to him only once, explaining myself, explaining him. Oh, it was a wonderful letter, the one wonderful letter of my life! I gave all I had to give in that letter, but it didn't seem to warm him at all, and I hadn't the heart or the energy to write again.

"He became a tender memory . . . and I fell in love again, Raymond. But not as with my stone image, oh no! This was the sort of man who didn't count except in that I loved him, or thought I did. He was really no more than the servant of my reaction against the stone image, and to serve me well he had to help me demolish all the castles of sentiment I had built around him. And the stoutest and most beautiful castle of all I had built around that funny little Welsh inn! The memory of our days there haunted me: it made everything else seem not worth while, and so I told myself that something must be done about that, else it looked to be spoiling my whole life with regrets. Nothing in the world repeats itself except regret—and, of course, sardines. And so, Raymond, I set my horse to that last castle, to crash into it recklessly, gallantly, and to stride and laugh about its halls with another man, who was not a stone image, not so beautiful.

"We went, my reaction and I. In an exceedingly fast car we went, going ever so fast, so that when I tumbled out of it at that inn I had had no time to think. Now the sweetest thing in that little inn was its miniature dining-room, which was entirely composed of a large bow window and three little tables; and the largest thing about it was the view of the hills all round, and a brown stream which tumbled about at the bottom of the garden and made more noise than you could believe possible for so little a thing. My stone image and I had sat at the table by the bow window, and now my reaction and I sat there again. I dreamed, he ate. My back was to the door, and I sat facing a large mirror, the stream and the hills on my right; he sat facing the window, adoring me, the adventure, the hills, the food. I wasn't unhappy; perhaps I was a little absent-minded, but I am sure I wasn't unhappy—until, in the mirror in front of me,

I saw the great figure, the fair hair, the frozen blue eyes, at the open door. Our eyes met in the mirror, the eyes of statues, wondering, waiting. . . .

"Shall I tell you I was afraid, or ashamed, or intolerably miserable? I don't know what I felt, it is a dead moment. I don't know how long he stood there, filling the doorway with his great figure, filling my life with his stern eyes. But it couldn't have been for long, perhaps a few seconds; and once he took his eyes off mine and looked at the man beside me, who hadn't seen him. I thought his lips twitched, but then something happened to my sight, and the mirror clouded over. When I could see again, the door was closed, the magic mirror was empty of all but my unbelieving eyes and the profile of the man beside me, who didn't know and was never to know that I had lived a century while he ate a potato.

"All that he did know was that the next morning I begged him to observe but not, please, to comment on my movements, which were in the direction of a London train. I treated that man abominably, abominably. But he never had a chance. . . . When I got home I found a wire. I had given orders for nothing, not even wires, to be sent on to me. This one had come an hour after I had left for Wales. It was from Southampton. 'Just arrived. Am going straight up to the little place in Wales. Will arrive there dinner-time. Shall we dine together by the window?'"

Shelmerdene was rather absent-minded as she finished her story; she forgot to smile. It was very careless of Shelmerdene to forget to smile, for it made Raymond Paris feel shy; he fiddled with his pen; he coughed.

"Well," said Shelmerdene, at last, "won't that story do for you, Raymond? Or is it not interesting enough? Not enough action?"

"Of course, it's frightfully interesting," Raymond Paris protested. "But—well, you see, editors are rather odd. It isn't a story at all, really, don't you see. . . ."

"An episode, perhaps?"

The young man started at a certain quality in her voice; something seemed to have suddenly broken in Shelmerdene's voice. Wondering, he stared at the lady who stood above him by the table, her fingers playing thoughtfully with the ancient pink shagreen cigarette-case, which had once been vanity-box in chief to Marie Antoinette, so they said. And he followed her eyes out of the window into the garden below, the garden brave with the gay tall tulips of many colours. A man was walking in the garden, not heeding the tulips, not heeding anything, the back of a great figure of a man with a golf-bag swung across it, a lounging man with hands stuck very deep into plus-fours and a pipe screwed into the corner of his mouth; and the tall man's hair was extraordinarily fair in the sunlight. George Tarlyon was walking through the garden of tulips on his way to a morning round of golf.

"Yes, an episode, that's all it is," said Shelmerdene queerly, and still her face forgot to smile. "That's how he would think of it now. He has had his lesson, you see—and many episodes! And so all the childishness has gone out of him. . . . He can't be hurt by a face in a mirror now, Raymond! He would just laugh, and he has an eighteenth-century kind of laugh. Poor lamb, all the childishness has been spilled out of him."

And Shelmerdene's eyes softly followed the figure among the tall tulips, while young Raymond Paris murmured: "You see, what editors want is a story with some sort of point. . . ."

# When the Nightingale Sang
# in Berkeley Square

There is a tale that is told in London about a nightingale, how it did this and that and, finally, for no apparent reason, rested and sang in Berkeley Square. A well-known poet, critic, and commentator heard it, and it is further alleged that he was sober. Some men, of course, now say that it was not a nightingale at all, but only the South wind singing in the trees of the square, but it is a fact that some men will say anything. And some men have formed a Saint James's Square school of thought, but it was in Berkeley Square that the poet, critic, and commentator, who was sober, distinctly heard the song of the nightingale, on a night in the heart of the drought of the year 1921.

In the drawing-room of a house midway on the entailed side of the square sat a lady and a gentleman silently. Or rather, the lady lay, while the gentleman sat, and the sofa on which she lay was far from the arm-chair in which he sat. The room was spacious; four shaded candles in tall candle-sticks of ancient brass gave calm colour to its dimness; and four open windows, from which the curtains were withdrawn in slack folds of shining silver, gave out to the leaves of the trees, which murmured among themselves just a little.

At last the gentleman roused himself from the gloom of his chair in the recess of the room, and threw back his head and stretched his arms so that little things cracked behind his shoulders. But the lady did not stir nor look round at him, she lay still on the sofa by the windows, her head deep in the hollow of a crimson cushion, her eyes thoughtfully on the ceiling, which was high enough to refuse itself to exact scrutiny in the affected light of four candles.

The gentleman drew a cigar-case from his breast pocket, and a cigar from the case. He bit the cigar, and then he moved, to deposit what he had bitten from the tip of his finger into an ash-tray. Then he lit his cigar, thoughtfully, and he said: "Hell, it's hot!"

"Perhaps, dear, it's a rehearsal for same," said the lady.

"I shouldn't wonder," he said, and stood with his back to the great Adam fireplace, and smoked his cigar. He was of medium-height, weathered looking, and broadly set: getting a little stout lately, and his fair hair thinning at the top. A commonplace face, you might call it, but the nose was good: straight, short and sensitive, very English. This was Ralph Loyalty, whose aunt, the late "John Loyalty," had delighted our fathers with her books, which were of the sentimental-sophisticated sort and have now dated a good deal. Ralph Loyalty was more than usually happy in his aunt, for she had left him a fortune, a famous name, but, people said, only the more solid side of her good sense. He was a man who liked the company of men; his recreations were golf, joining clubs, auction-bridge, and dining with his wife; he enjoyed George Robey, and he admired other people's brains. Some people thought him rather solid and unimaginative—"estimable qualities," they said, "but rather heavy on the hand." But, as "Ralph" in half a dozen clubs meant Ralph Loyalty, other people said that popularity was his form of genius, and they were probably right. He was said to be in love with his wife. He tolerated rakes, cads, and co-respondents among his acquaintance, but he never understood them. Effeminate men he laughed at rather shyly, and left it at that. He had no enemies, but most of his wife's friends disliked him. They would have been surprised to see him at this moment, so miserable he looked, but they would not have been surprised at his wife's attitude on the sofa, for naturally she was bored to death with the man. His wife's friends had long since despaired of Ralph Loyalty ever seeing that his wife was bored to death with him, and that is why they would have been surprised to see him now, for it was obviously because he had realised that this evening, at last, that he looked so miserable.

"Well . . ." began Ralph Loyalty suddenly, and then very deliberately knocked the ash of his cigar into the fireplace, which was unlike him with an ash-tray at hand, for he was an orderly man. And then he said a wicked word and banged out of the room. The candles flickered madly in the sudden draught.

But it was as though Mrs. Loyalty did not hear the crash of the door, she did not stir. She did not sigh, nor did she instantly light a match for the cigarette which had lain for many minutes forgotten near her hand.

Joan Loyalty was dark, or rather her hair was dark, and darker than ever against the crimson cushion. But her face was fair, English fair; and many generations had gone to the establishing of her complexion and the exact shaping of her delicate aquiline nose. But it was her eyes that were important, to the student of such things. Joan Loyalty belonged to the society of the day, and of that society her face, the oval sort, was, her friends said in their loose way, in the best way "typical." She was of the type early twentieth century, but her gestures, and lack of them, were ancient enough, for they were fully expressive of that which really differentiates men from beasts, the social quality of being tired. But beneath that manner, that classical insolence which is inadequately called affectation, lay a Joan who was as sudden and as simple as the first woman. And that is why her eyes were important, to the student of such things, for in them was that thing which defies the analysing of novelists and demagogues, the thoughtful look which may only be thinking of a walk in a field with a dog and a stick, the curious, absent look which can smell the sea from a long way off.

At last Mrs. Loyalty lit her cigarette, and she rose from the sofa, and for a few minutes she listened to the murmuring of the leaves in the square; and then she crossed the dimness of the room to a bell-button, and pressed it.

Smith came, and she said:

"Downstairs in the study you will find a book, probably on the small table by the window. A slim, blue book, by a Mr. Beerbohm. Please bring it to me."

The shadow of Smith hovered doubtfully among the shadows by the door.

"Mr. Loyalty is in the study, madam, and told me he was not to be disturbed."

"Ah," said Mrs. Loyalty softly. And she smiled, and when she smiled you understood why dogs liked her at once.

"All right, Smith," she said. "I will fetch it myself."

The shadow of Smith vanished in a flickering of candles, but Mrs. Loyalty did not follow him at once. She stood where Ralph Loyalty had stood, with her back to the great Adam fireplace; in a gesture of tired thought she clasped her hands behind her head, and from the motionless cigarette between her lips the smoke floated upwards without a curve until it faded, for she was forgetting to draw it. Then, suddenly, she dropped the half-smoked cigarette into the empty grate, an untidy habit of hers with which her husband could not ever quite overlook, and left the room.

The quality of silence was very noticeable about the figure of Mrs. Loyalty: it had been favourably commented on by distinguished foreigners, who say that though foreign women are noisy talkers, Englishwomen are noisy walkers; which, however, sounds like a generalisation, and should be mistrusted as such.

But silence was, in a particular way, a quality of Mrs. Loyalty's figure, just like its slimness. And when, a few minutes later, she re-entered the room with her book in her hand, it was almost as though she had not re-entered the room or had never left it;

perhaps a shadow faintly stirred among the shadows by the door, but the draught of her coming in did not seem to disturb the sensitive light of the candles.

She moved one of them to the little table at the head of the sofa, she sat against the crimson cushion, and she read her book. But minutes passed and she did not turn over the page, so perhaps she was just pretending to read. Minutes passed, and then the light of the candles writhed across her page, and she looked up to see a great disturbance among the shadows by the door. She stared with very wide eyes at the dark apparition there, and her hand went to her heart in a still way she had, and she sighed curiously. The apparition came forward, and she stared at it with almost unbelieving eyes.

"Joan," the apparition said, "I never thought I should live to see you look frightened!" A gay voice, rather shy.

He stood before her, a tall, very thin man, stooping a little, with feverish dark eyes set in a notably ascetic face, which had gained for him the comical name of "The Metaphysician." His face was as though a fever lay behind it, a kind of sombre restlessness, but every now and then it would twitch into a shy smile; his face looked as though it had suffered much pain, but had never got used to pain. He smiled down at her intimately, but also shyly, which made the smile very attractive.

"Well," she said up to him softly, "you did come in rather like a ghost, didn't you?" She seemed to examine him.

"Didn't Ralph tell you I was coming?"

That seemed to surprise her, but she only shook her head slightly.

"I saw Ralph at the club this evening and told him I might look in," he added.

"He didn't tell me," she said. "But why didn't you let *me* know?"

"You see, Joan," said Hugo Carr, "I've had as much as I can bear of this hole-and-corner business." A shy way Mr. Carr had; he would say firm things in a very shy voice, with the fever always behind his face. That's what makes him attractive to women, people said. "Hugo lays down the law," once said George Tarlyon, "as though he were laying eggs and was afraid they might break."

He sat down on the sofa beside her, very close; on the edge of the sofa, sideways to her, with one knee almost on the ground. She lit a cigarette: and, seeing the appeal on his face, she smiled a little, her lips smiled, and she said softly:

"Forgive me, dear, but I feel very silent. The heat, perhaps. But go on with your speech—please do! And I'm hoping, too, that it will contain some inside information as to why you have not been to see me or even rung me up for a week. It's such bad luck for a woman," she said softly, "when a man of honour remembers his honour. Don't you think so, Hugo?"

Her eyes looked as though she had left them on guard somewhere, watching something for her. But he didn't notice that. He was one of those feverish men who never notice anything but other people's feverishness, at which they feel aggrieved.

"See, Joan," he began nervously. "You and I have been living a lie for two years. There's no getting out of it—for two whole years! We've drugged ourselves and each other with saying we couldn't help it—"

"*You* have," she murmured. "I don't need drugs."

"Yes, *I* have," he agreed quickly. "And you have let me. Because there was nothing we could do—so we said." And suddenly he broke off, and put his hand on her knee. "Do you love me, Joan?"

"Yes," she said, no more, for Joan's love was never expressed in words, she was not like that. But it was his particular effeminacy, to be intensely pleased to hear her say she loved him. He would glow, *de profundis*. One of two people in love must be effeminate, after all.

"That's been my one excuse," he said shyly. "And it's my justification now for what I must do—that we've loved each other for two years, and still love each other. I'm going to ask Ralph to-night to give you your freedom. . ."

"So that's why you haven't been to see me for a week!"

"Yes. I wanted to be free to think. You influence me frightfully, Joan, you're stronger than I am, and so if I was to think our way out of this muddle I had to do it alone. Ralph was my best friend. And for two years you and I have been meeting each other secretly for lunch and for the afternoons, and at home you've been living this lie with Ralph. You've sort of crucified yourself, Joan, because you didn't want to hurt Ralph. And I've let you! It's ghastly. And Ralph has always trusted us together, he's made it easy for us. It's ghastly, Joan."

"Yes, it's ghastly," she murmured from her heart.

"Joan," her lover whispered, "in the secret book in which our lives are being written, you will appear as an angel and I as a cad. For that is how it has been for two years . . ." And Hugo Carr of the sombre eyes and the thin face that looked as though a fever lay behind it passed a hand across his eyes; and her arm crept up round his shoulder, and she held his face very near.

"Poor darling!" she whispered. "You've suffered frightfully, haven't you?" And she did little things to comfort him.

"But you've suffered much more," he whispered into her hair. He kissed her hair. "And I've let you—go on not *hurting* Ralph! And what good has it done? Ralph suspects me. I know he does. It's difficult to explain. . ."

"But it will be all right now," Joan soothed his wretchedness.

He turned her face to him and looked into her eyes, the grave eyes that looked as though she had left them on guard somewhere, watching something for her.

"So you do agree with me now, Joan?" he whispered gladly.

But she seemed to answer irrelevantly, with a peculiar little laugh she had, which stabbed his heart with a pleasure that was almost pain.

"To agree or to disagree—what does it matter to me, Hugo! Only you matter, sitting here. And I only matter because I am beside you. So let's be silent a little while, thinking of each other. . . ."

And she turned very wretched eyes on him.

"Do you realise, Hugo, that you and I have scarcely had a minute of silence together for two years—you and I, whose lives are spent in chattering, have had to go on chattering even when we were alone, we could never forget ourselves or Ralph, we had always to be discussing what we would do and how we would do it and when we would do it. Discussing and discussing and discussing! Oh, dear, our love has been one endless discussion! And we are not very young any more, my sweet! But now we will be just silent, thinking of nothing but each other—for the first time in two years, we won't think of Ralph, my dear, we just won't! To please me, Hugo. . . ."

It was an unusual pleasure for him to see her so soft, she who was so essentially *fine* that her natural softness had been merged into a great calmness: a delicious thing in a woman, calmness, but rather frightening.

But this was a matter of honour to-night. He had betrayed his best friend for two years, and would not betray him any longer. It had come to a point of honour that he must tell Ralph Loyalty that he loved Joan. And so now, even as he thrilled at her sweetness, he would have liked to say to her that his business to-night was with a point of honour, but he was much too self-conscious to be dramatic. He smiled self-consciously, and only said:

"But I must see Ralph to-night, dear. When I came in I told Smith—"

"Oh!" she cut impatiently in. "Be silent, Hugo, be silent—let's enjoy ourselves while we may!" Nerves, of course. As herself admitted immediately by asking, quite differently: "What did you say you told Smith? Didn't he just tell you I was up here alone?"

"Yes. But I asked where Ralph was, and he said in the study, and so I told him to tell Ralph in an hour's time that I was here. He said Ralph had given orders not to be disturbed, but I told him he expected me—and so I suppose he'll be here soon."

"Ah," sighed Joan.

"God, it will be difficult!" Hugo muttered. "Dear old Ralph—the simplest man there ever was! What an unholy mess life is, Joan—that you and I have to fight our way to happiness over Ralph's body, just because you met him before you met me!"

"Don't say that!" she cried sharply.

"Nerves," she smiled away his bewilderment.

"What I really meant was, don't say anything. For if you told Smith to tell him in an hour's time we've still half an hour or so together—" She held up her wrist to the candlelight— "yes, just about that, and then there will be quite enough talking and discussing. And I've got something important to tell you, too, before he comes in—but, dear, I must enjoy just a little peace before the storm that will set me free, my first bit of peace in two years." She pleaded with him, and it was delicious to hear Joan pleading, she who was usually so calm and sensible. And so they sat very close, hand in hand, like children.

But Smith's idea of an hour was influenced by a not unnatural desire to go to bed; and they had not enjoyed their peace for more than five minutes when it was tremendously shattered by footfalls on the stairs.

"Oh, Lord!" muttered Hugo Carr. But rather comically, for, after all, it had to be got over some time.

Joan went queerly taut, and began to say something, very swiftly, but the door opened just then and he did not catch what it was.

Entered Smith—only Smith! And Hugo Carr breathed relief that his point of honour had not yet grown a point. Joan made no sign.

Smith came forward quickly. The candles flickered uneasily across his face. He addressed Hugo Carr.

"Sir," he said quickly, "I went in to announce you to Mr. Loyalty—" He broke off, and his eyes hovered over Joan.

"Yes, Smith?" she encouraged him softly.

Smith's eyes still hovered about her, he seemed very perturbed. He addressed the air between them.

"Mr. Loyalty's dead," said Smith.

Smith was not a heartless man. He was moved, and plunged again into the startled silence: "I went in and found him with his head laid across the writing-table and a little bottle empty by his hand. I shook 'im. . ."

"My God!" muttered Hugo Carr. But still his eyes were fixed on Smith, he could not look at Joan.

An analysis of suicide was not among Smith's duties. He only added: "I have telephoned to Dr. Gay, madam, and as he was out playing bridge I asked Mrs. Gay to ring him up to come here, as it was very urgent." Wise Smith! What could be more non-committal than "very urgent" for suicide?

"My God!" muttered Hugo Carr—and jumped up and strode away to the fireplace. He had not yet looked at Joan.

But Smith looked at her, and she back at him. Smith was a nice man, and he respected his mistress immensely, her *kind*.

"I am very sorry indeed, madam," said Smith. Joan's lips scarcely moved.

"Thank you, Smith."

Smith went out softly.

"I never dreamt—" Hugo Carr burst out, then choked. It was as though he had swept his arm round to ward off an intolerable thing and had found the thing too intolerable.

Joan went to him.

"Hugo," she awoke him softly. And he looked at her for the first time since Smith's entrance, his eyes clung to her. A very fond gesture took her hand to his shoulder—the tall, thin, stooping man whose white face took a word as visibly as it suffered a headache. Hugo Carr found many things quite unbearable.

His eyes seemed to cling to her for a support against his thoughts.

"It's ghastly," he whispered. "Joan, don't you see—it's ghastly! Poor old Ralph—down there, all alone! While we up here"— He passed a hand over his mouth to stop its twitching; and it was as though his hand had put on it a bitterness which was not there before. "While we up here were making love—his best friend and his wife!"

Involuntarily he put the best friend first, for Hugo Carr loved his friends; and, for him, friendship was one of the first principles of the civilised state. That is how he saw the civilised state.

"Poor, poor Ralph!" she said ever so softly.

His eyes tore away from her face. As though they hadn't been able to find there the support they needed.

"There are some things . . ." he began feverishly.

"Oh, my dear!" Joan protested miserably, as though against the unbearable philosophy of it. But it is a mistake to protest against the unbearable philosophy of a man of honour.

"There are some things," Mr. Carr insisted with feverish violence, "that are unpardonable and unmendable. And there's no excuse big enough for them. . ."

He looked like a priest, a priest in the temple of friendship, burning incense to the ideal idea . . . And Joan nodded, her eyes on him who saw nothing but the ruin of the ideal idea.

"God simply has not put enough excuses into the world to meet the crimes of the world." The words burst out of him. "And this is even worse, because it is a crime so big that there's simply no punishment been made to meet it. It's just betrayal . . ." And the force of that mediæval word, its ultimate meaning, broke him down. Hugo Carr sobbed.

"O my God, it's beastly, beastly! Poor old Ralph, down in that room, alone. Betrayed—by his best friend and his wife—and suspecting at last that he had been betrayed, only suspecting it—and not able to bear the suspicion. That's the horrible part of it—don't you see, Joan, don't you see? How could he bear it—dear old Ralph, who has never suspected any one in his life? He simply wasn't made that way. And so . . . Oh, my God, while we were making love up here, we who've quibbled for two years whether we would hurt his feelings or not—his *feelings*! We've killed old Ralph . . ."

Her eyes were on him, but he saw nothing but the ruin of the ideal idea, and an odd little curve crept about her mouth. Perhaps it was from an odd little curve like that about the lips of a young princess of olden time that there sprang the many tales of young princesses who loved yet lashed their lovers. It was not contemptuous, it was much too little a curve for that. It was supremely dignified. Monna Lisa has it, though some say that Monna Lisa smiles. If Mary Stuart had seen the portrait of Monna Lisa she would have whispered: "She is thinking that men are but minutes in a woman's life, and she is right."

"Hugo!"

But when he looked at her it was as though he was still looking at ruins.

"It is not fair to us to say we've killed him. And it's childish. Life killed him, Hugo! And you are not more sorry than I—who have tried so hard for eight years to make life sweet for him. Oh, my God, how I've tried!"

He thought out aloud, softly: "You are a marvellous woman, Joan!"

"It's only," she said gently, "that I know what is worth while to me and you don't. That must make life very difficult for you . . ." That is all she said, and Hugo Carr stared at her, bewilderment joining the fever in his eyes.

"What do you mean, Joan?" he asked, miserably bewildered. Hugo Carr couldn't bear not understanding things.

A few yards separated them; and Joan crossed swiftly to him, and she took his arm and held it very tight. Some people said that Joan's hands were almost too thin, but what they held they held very tightly.

"Listen to me, Hugo—for if this mood of yours isn't met now, in this horrible moment, it may ruin our lives—"

"*May* ruin!" But she held his arm tight.

"Yes, dear, this is ruin—but why won't you face facts, why won't you face the bogey that life has shaped to frighten us, why won't you see that this is the culminating point of three ruined lives and that on the ruins of three lives we must now build a city for two? It won't be a very fair city, Hugo, but it's ours by right, by the only real right in this wrong world—the right of misery . . ."

Now the eyes of a man who sees a wraith are more frightening than the wraith that he sees. That is why Joan Loyalty left her sentence in the air, for it had been snapped by his stare.

"But aren't you—sorry?" he whispered dryly.

And she laughed—her nerves laughed through her mouth.

"Sorry! *You* dare to ask me if I am sorry! Oh, Hugo, is it absolutely necessary for the love of a man for a woman to be expressed in fatuous questions? Oh, God, what kind of thing is this love that it tricks a mind into loving a man!"

"I don't know what you mean . . ." he muttered sulkily. Hugo Carr couldn't bear not understanding things.

"You ask me if I am sorry—I, who have lived through a hell of boredom for eight years so as not to hurt Ralph's feelings, not to break his heart! And now at last it's broken. Yes, I am sorry. Frightfully sorry. And I am also glad—I feel as though I myself had died and that my soul had been freed from a long imprisonment. That is what I felt, as though it was I who was dead, when I saw him—"

He gaped at her idiotically.

"For Heaven's sake don't stare in that idiotic way, Hugo! I've already had more than I can bear to-night, sitting here and thinking and thinking of poor Ralph downstairs and wondering what final thought it must have been that made him do it—"

Hugo Carr couldn't understand. "But when—how?"

Had not she warned him that she had already had more than she could bear? And now her nerves rose up to meet his gaping stare.

"That is why I looked so frightened when you came in—I didn't expect you, I didn't know who it could be, and I was afraid. And that is why I was relieved when you said you had told Smith to go into the study in an hour's time—because that would give me time to think, to realise the thing, and to tell you. Didn't I say that I had something important to tell you before—before Ralph came in? I was going to tell you that Ralph would never come in, for I had seen him when I went downstairs to fetch a book—"

"You were reading when I came in!" he accused her queerly.

"Oh, dear, you are like a man out of every book that was ever written by men about women! I was pretending to read. And then you told me you had come to see Ralph on a point of honour! At last you had summoned up your courage to see Ralph—on a point of honour. And that's why I wanted you to be silent for a while, for speech sometimes makes a tragedy unbearably idiotic. I wanted peace, Hugo! I wanted just to taste the peace between the old life and the new, the old life in which there was no honour and the new life in which there will anyway be happiness . . ." And she touched him, but with a blind gesture of his arm he swept her aside, and strode out of the room. She stared, wide-eyed, unrealising, at the panels of the door; she took two quick steps towards the door, she stopped, and then she ran madly to it and opened it and called

"Hugo, Hugo!" But, even as she cried his name, the door below slammed massively, like a knell from the bowels of the earth; and through the windows of the room behind her came the noise of swift footsteps striding away . . .

She went back into the room. Still she could not realise. She paced about the room, here, there, trying to think, trying not to think, wishing to give way to the intolerable moment, unable to give way. The candles danced furiously in the gentle draught, for she had left the door wide open. She was but a shadow among a furious company of shadows—when, as she was by the windows, she saw one more in the open doorway. She screamed behind her teeth.

"I heard you call his name," said Ralph Loyalty hoarsely from the door. "Have you quarrelled? D'you mean to say he's gone for good?"

He came towards her as he spoke. But this was not the Ralph she knew, this was not the Ralph who had lived and died, this was a man with a furious face. He advanced on her. Her knees trembled, and she would have fallen but for a hand on the back of the sofa.

"D'you mean to say he's gone for good?" he repeated again furiously. She nodded dumbly. She was going to faint.

Then Ralph Loyalty said a wicked word. "D'you mean to say that I've been shamming dead in a damned uncomfortable position for the last two hours for nothing?" he bawled at her. "Here have I been for months and months throwing you at each other's heads and neither of you with the pluck to show your hand!" And he cursed the name of Hugo Carr for the name of a fool and a coward. She was going to faint. He controlled himself a little. He appealed to her. "I didn't want to hurt your feelings, you see, Joan. I knew how you'd loved me for years, and I couldn't bear to hurt you, but I'd have given anything to let you see I wanted my freedom to marry some one else. And when I saw that you liked being with Hugo I thought there might be a chance of your liking him instead of me, and so I did my best to throw you together. But Hugo always was a coward—and as I couldn't bear going on as we were for another night I arranged this thing to-night, thinking that if anything would make Hugo show his hand or would throw you into Hugo's arms, this would." And again he said a wicked word. "I didn't want to hurt you, you see, Joan, and so I thought this would be the best way—and now the silly ass has gone and left us stranded . . ."

That was the night the nightingale sang in Berkeley Square. A nightingale has never sung in Berkeley Square before, and may never sing there again, but if it does it will probably *mean* something.

# The Hunter after Wild Beasts

## I

Out of his loneliness Aubrey Carlyle told me this story one night: not at Malmanor Park, where, with his sister Esther as hostess, he has entertained us all so often, for he said that he could not have told me this story at Malmanor, but in the library of his house in London.

Aubrey Carlyle, who is a man of middle years, had never told this story to any one before, and I can only think he told it to me because I had been a great friend to his wife Gloria. I have not seen Gloria Carlyle for three years, though I have very often wished to, for she is a lady of uncommon quality and was a very loyal friend. Of her George Tarlyon once said that she was a gentleman among women; "and that is a very rare thing," added Shelmerdene, "for the only advantage most women have over men is in the fact that they are not gentlemen." But that is as it may be.

The last I heard of Gloria Carlyle was that she had settled in Italy and was living in a villa near Florence. And I saw a vision of Gloria in a very white villa among the myrtle and magnolia and waxen camellias of that country, and walking in lanes where green lizards moved swiftly up gray stone walls—dear Gloria of the tiger-tawny hair and the funny crooked smile like a naughty fairy's! She was a very sweet and thoughtful woman, and her voice never, never intruded, it was like a hidden stream, quite delicious. . . .

Aubrey Carlyle told me that I could tell or write this story as I wished, saying that it might better the knowledge of men about their womenfolk; "for there are too many men," he said, "who do not know their jobs as regards their women. And I have learnt mine too late."

My friend Aubrey is a man of an aloof and almost haughty demeanour, which may have perhaps induced that rather abrupt manner that has repelled many people from him; for though a certain aloofness was thought very proper to the looks of an English gentleman of a past time, it is now held to be quite out of place among the corrupt genialities of the democratic state. A tall, dark-looking man he was, and elegant in a tweedy sort of way. Rich always, he had never been a wastrel, and London bored him to distraction—or "to distinction," as an American out of Texas once said. A Tory landlord of Liberal sympathies, he was always a model administrator of his properties; and chief among these we, their friends, counted Gloria, for she seemed—how can one suggest these shades of understanding?—more particularly and peculiarly his wife than are the wives of less fortunate men. It is said of the Carlyles that they have always been bad to their women and that there has been no charge on the female estate for more than two hundred years; but Aubrey and Gloria were a charming couple. It was always quite evident that she loved him—tall Gloria of the tiger-tawny hair and the funny crooked smile like a naughty fairy's; while it was equally evident—to those few, of course, who could look beneath the aloof surface of the man—that he treasured her enormously. And then, one day, she left him; and she never came back.

Now Aubrey despised what he called the "trumpery parlour-tricks" of the countryside. He was not civilised enough, he said. The elegant pastime of killing a pretty fowl of the air without any risk to yourself, or of chasing a scared fox across a county—though that was better, for you at least risked a broken collar-bone—did not amuse him very much. He was a hunter after wild beasts. And because you may not kill wild beasts in England, for they walk on two legs and stern laws protect them, the other four continents knew Aubrey Carlyle for many months in the year. And because Gloria was not a hunter after wild beasts she stayed in England, and was much with us in London, and we sometimes with her at Malmanor. But she was an amazingly still woman.

The war came, and Aubrey was very happy at his pastime, legalised at last, in Flanders, and grew to be a brigadier. And Gloria grew to be a woman, for she had somehow seemed very young until then. The war gasped to conclusion, and soon Aubrey was in South America, in the darkness beyond the upper reaches of the Amazon. And when, one evening, he returned to Malmanor, he found that Gloria was gone.

## II

In the vast hall-way of the house, with men tramping about the stone floor bringing in his luggage and his trophies, the butler very silently gave him a slim letter. Aubrey Carlyle looked at the handwriting on the letter, and then at the silent servant.

"When did my wire arrive?"

"At six o'clock last night, sir."

And then Aubrey knew the letter in his hand to hold the greatest shock of his life. But he was not a dramatic man, he did not take his surprises dramatically. He put the letter into his pocket.

"And then, Hunt?"

"Sir?"

"And then?"

"Madam left by the eleven o'clock London train this morning, sir. She took luggage."

"I will have a bath now. Very hot, tell Vesey. Dinner at the usual time. Thank you, Hunt." Twenty-five years had Hunt been with his master; ten years longer than Gloria.

Aubrey had his bath, very hot. And then he put on those nice, slack, black things which so advantage a man's looks at night; and with them he always wore a soft shirt, for Aubrey would have seen the greatest hostess in the land to blazes rather than be uncomfortable in a stiff one. For a long time he sat on the broad window-seat in his bedroom and looked out on the avenue of tall trees that joined his park to the distant shroud of Carmion Wood. The prospect was very fair in the soft evening light. God is like a woman in the evenings, He makes the land look so shy. And then he heard Gloria's voice, but it was very distant, for it came from across a wide valley. He just heard Gloria's voice, but he could not make out what she was saying. And he remembered sudden little phrases of hers in her fine, whispering voice, little broken phrases, and how she would smile very crookedly, and how her great eyes would queerly cloud over.

And then he read the letter. It was a very short letter.

It was after ten o'clock when he passed from the dining-room into the drawing-room. Hunt entered after him to draw the curtains across the French windows, but he was told to let them be; and Hunt switched on the lights, but he was told to switch them off again and that nothing more would be required of him that night.

Again Aubrey read the letter. It was a very short letter. "You know why, dear. Good-bye. Gloria."

He was angry, because he didn't know why; he had not the faintest idea why. But anger is no sort of a weapon with which to fight solitude, and this was the most solitary moment of Aubrey Carlyle's life, he who had hunted wild beasts in the loneliest places of the Americas.

He threw wide open the three French windows and prowled about the large dim room. "You know why." God in Heaven, what was she talking about! How could he know why?—and what was there to know? He prowled about the room. . . .

They had been good friends, amazingly good friends. He had relied on her to understand that. Good Lord, everything he had done to her or had not done to her had been in friendship! Surely she had understood that. . . . She had seemed to. . . . Fourteen, fifteen years. . . . Why, she couldn't have expected him to behave like an impassioned lover all the time! Fifteen years. . . . There were moments. . . . When he came back from any of his travels and saw her, he loved her madly. It was like a choke in the heart when he saw her on his returns, that marvellous tawny Gloria with the funny crooked smile. Oh, child, child, what have you done? He had treated her like a friend. . . . And what was the use of having a great friend if you had to write letters to her? He never wrote letters when he was abroad, he hated writing letters. Of course she had understood that. . . .

And he prowled about the large dim room, through the clear throbbing stillness, for the face of the moon hung over distant Carmion Wood and leered genially into the room. He did not understand. . . . At last he sat down in a great chair by the fire-place, and as he sat there he thought how, after his many returns, he had sat on that chair and taken Gloria to his knee and loved her. And Aubrey Carlyle cried for the first time in his life. . . .

### III

He sat there, a very solitary man, and his eyes wandered vaguely through the open windows over the bewitched countryside, his gardens and his park and his acres and his forests, shrouded all in a clear gloom as though God was peering at them in the light of a taper. And the heavy moon climbed the heavens. He saw the twisted shapes of tall flowers in the garden, flowers he did not know, for his head-gardener was a man of invention in August. And then, among the tall shapes of the August flowers, he saw one in particular, and this one was the tallest among them, and it moved. But he sat very still and solemn in his chair, watching the shape of the moving flower, between him and the heavy moon. And then it wavered and stood; for a long time it stood, a shadow in the wan countryside. Perhaps it was afraid, all alone there among the flowers. He watched. And then it was framed in the open window, a soft slim shadow. But he did not move.

"What sort of a play is this," he heard his voice ask, "in which a woman goes away like a coward and comes back like a wraith?"

And into the room she came, and with a sigh she sat down in a chair by the window.

"Oh, dear!" she sighed. "I am so tired. . ."

His heart was so torn with gladness that for a long time he could not move, he could not speak. And then he walked across the room and stood above her chair. She turned up her little face under the tiger-tawny hair and smiled her funny crooked smile like a naughty fairy's.

"Poor Aubrey!" she whispered. "Poor Gloria!. . ."

But he did not touch her.

"Listen, Gloria," he whispered. "When I found you had gone, my life cracked like an earthenware cup . . ." And Aubrey Carlyle stopped, amazed by what he had said; for he had never said a thing like that before.

"And now," he said, "you have mended it again."

"Have I?" she cried queerly; and the weight of her eyes on him bore him to his knees by her chair. He had not seen her for eight months, but still he did not touch her.

"And *my* life, Aubrey?"

"But your life is mine, Gloria! We are together!"

And Gloria, the soft, lovely Gloria smiled into his absorbed face. . . .

"Of course," she said. "Of course! An Englishman and his wife. . . ."

But he was not listening.

"And did you know why, Aubrey?" she asked.

He shook his head. He had not seen her for eight months.

"I just thought you had gone mad, Gloria. Tell me, are you mad?"

"No, dear; I am very sane. And very tired." And she said that in a voice which seemed to come from the depths of a very deep bowl, the softest voice that a man ever heard, and it broke the poise of his restraint. He had not seen her for eight months. He was very strong, and a lawless man. He carried her away into the depths of the room. She said nothing.

## IV

And then, again, they were by the open windows. But a cloud with a satin fringe hid the moon, and it was so dark that the shine of her eyes was all he could see of her face. And Gloria was so tall that her eyes were almost level with his.

"And so you didn't know why, in my letter?" she asked miserably.

He humoured her. . . .

"Well, why?"

"You hunt wild beasts, don't you, Aubrey?"

"And I bring the skins for you to walk on, Gloria."

"And when you come back from your hunting, you ravage me like a wild beast—"

He cried out sharply in amazement, but she went on, like a sibyl:

"And then you go away again. And then again you come back, to ravage me—"

"Gloria, you are mad!"

"No, I am very sane. And very tired. I loved you, Aubrey. I shall never love any one else. I am clotted with your passions, Aubrey. I wanted love, but you ravaged me like a wild beast. And what is left of me now, I want to preserve. Oh, I want to! *Please* understand . . . just a little! All last night I wondered what I would do. I saw you coming back, my dear, the hunter coming back to his fireside and his wife and his holiday—oh, yes, I am your holiday, Aubrey!—and then I saw you going away again, leaving me. . . . Oh, Aubrey, how you have sinned against love! And so I went away, because of the horror of it. And I have come back, because of the horror of your loneliness. I, who am used to loneliness! And I also came back to see if you were—different. . . ."

"If," she whispered, "we were living in a past time, I should go into a nunnery, to get assoiled. But as it is, dear, I shall go for a walk. . . ."

"Let me come with you," he begged humbly.

"No, Aubrey. I'd like to walk quite alone. Towards the moon and back." But the moon was behind a cloud with a satin fringe.

He watched her as she walked across the garden and was lost in darkness. He waited for a long time, but he knew she would not return. She has never returned.

# The Man with the Broken Nose

## I

"Ever been to the National Gallery?" asked George Tarlyon. It was an offensive question to ask a grown man, but I answered it.

"Ah," said Tarlyon.

"I can't help thinking," said Tarlyon, "that you did Madam Tussaud's the same afternoon. . . ."

"If you want to know, it was the Tower, St. Paul's, and the National Gallery that I did on the same afternoon. My mother took me."

"Of course, I can't compete with your mother," said Tarlyon; "but I will take you—now. Waiter—the bill, please."

It was a day in July, and we were sitting over luncheon at the Café Royal. It was very warm for the time of the year. I don't know if I have mentioned it, but I am something in the City. There was, if you remember, a slump in the City in the summer of 1922. I was in that slump. And so, what with one thing and another, I sighed. . . .

"Come on," said Tarlyon firmly. "One must not neglect art. And two certainly mustn't." Poor, silly man!

We walked from the Café Royal to Trafalgar Square, which is an untidy walk on a glaring afternoon in July. And then we walked about the Gallery; we looked at paintings with that rapt look which can see All Round and Into a thing; and we stood before "Musidora Bathing her Feet."

"What a masterpiece," Tarlyon sighed, "if only she hadn't got three legs!" I could not at first see Musidora's third leg, but after he had pointed it out to me I could see nothing else but that ghostly third leg dangling over her knee between the other two.

"You see," he explained, "Gainsborough painted one leg badly, and so he painted it out and fitted another—but Musidora's third leg came back. Say what you like, there is something displeasing about a woman with an exaggerated number of legs, though some people rather like that kind of thing, saying that a woman can't have too many. . . ."

It was as we turned away, talking loftily about legs, that we were confronted by a tall and dark young man.

"Sir," he addressed Tarlyon, "I would be obliged if you would tell me in which gallery hang the pictures by Manet?"

One wondered why he didn't ask one of the many uniformed men who are strewn about the Gallery for the purpose of being asked that kind of thing.

"You are quite sure," Tarlyon put frankly to him, "that you do not mean Monet?"

"Manet," said the dark stranger, and looked as though he meant it.

"Well, then, you're in luck," said Tarlyon; "for we, too, were just about to view the Manets. We are partial to Manet. This way."

We followed him like lambs. Tarlyon's knowledge as to where the Manets were took the form of trying every gallery in which the Manets were not. We repassed Gainsborough's three-legged lady, Tarlyon commenting. The dark stranger walked silently but firmly. He was a tall young man of slight but powerful build; his nose, which was of the patrician sort, would have been shapely had it not once been broken in such a way that for ever after it must noticeably incline to one side; and, though his appearance was that of a gentleman, he carried himself with an air of determination and assurance which would, I thought, make any conversation with him rather a business. There was any amount of back-chat in his dark eyes. His hat, which was soft and had the elegance of the well-worn, he wore cavalierly. Shoes by Lobb.

At last a picture rose before our eyes, a large picture, very blue. Now who shall describe that picture which was so blue, blue even to the grass under the soldiers' feet, the complexion of the soldiers' faces and the rifles in the soldiers' hands? Over against a blue tree stood a man, and miserably blue was his face, while the soldiers stood very stiffly with their backs to us, holding their rifles in a position which gave one no room to doubt but that they were about to shoot the solitary man for some misdemeanour. He was the loneliest looking man I have ever seen.

"Manet," said Tarlyon.

The dark young stranger was absorbed; he pulled his hat a little lower over his left eye, so that the light should not obtrude on his vision. . . .

"Come on," I whispered to Tarlyon, for we seemed to be intruding—so that I was quite startled when the stranger suddenly turned from the picture to me.

"You see, sir," he said gravely, "I know all about killing. I have killed many men. . . ."

"Army Service Corps?" inquired Tarlyon.

"No, sir," snapped the stranger. "I know nothing of your Corps. I am a Zeytounli."

"Please have patience with me," I begged the stranger. "What is a Zeytounli?"

He regarded me with those smouldering dark eyes; and I realised vividly that his nose had been broken in some argument which had cost the other man more than a broken nose.

"Zeytoun," he said, "is a fortress in Armenia. For five hundred years Zeytoun has not laid down her arms, but now she is burnt stones on the ground. The Zeytounlis, sir, are the hill-men of Armenia. I am an Armenian."

"Oh, I'm so sorry," Tarlyon murmured.

"Why?" snarled the Armenian.

"Well, you've been treated pretty badly, haven't you?" said Tarlyon. "All these massacres and things. . . ."

The stranger glared at him, and then he laughed at him. I shall remember that laugh. So will Tarlyon. Then the stranger raised a finger and, very gently, he tapped Tarlyon's shoulder.

"Listen," said he. "Your manner of speaking bores me. Turks have slain many Armenians. Wherefore Armenians have slain many Turks. You may take it from me that, by sticking to it year in and year out for five hundred years, Armenians have in a tactful way slain more Turks than Turks have slain Armenians. That is why I am proud of being Armenian. And you would oblige me, gentlemen, by informing your countrymen that we have no use for their discarded trousers, which are anyway not so good in quality as they were, but would be grateful for some guns. And you would still further oblige me by trying, in future, not to talk nonsense about Armenians. Adieu, gentlemen. You will probably hear of me again. I am in England on public business."

He left us.

"I didn't know," I murmured, "that Armenians were like that. I have been misled about Armenians. And he speaks English very well. . . ."

"Hum," said Tarlyon thoughtfully. "But no one would say he was Armenian if he wasn't, would he?"

"Also," said I, "he is the most aggressive young man I have ever met. Manet indeed!"

"So would you be aggressive, if you had been massacred and made an atrocity of ever since you were a slip of a boy, and had spent your holidays being chased round Lake Van by roaring Turks and hairy Kurds with scimitars dripping with the blood of Circassian children."

"Oh, not Circassian!" I pleaded, for I have always been very sentimental about Circassian woman; but Tarlyon insisted that they generally died young and that they were a fat race. . . .

## II

This is what actually happened, towards midnight of that very day, within a stone's-throw of Claridge's Hotel, in Brook Street, Mayfair. George Tarlyon and I had been of the same company for dinner and then bridge at a house in Brook Street. Towards midnight a gap in the bridge allowed us to slip away, which we did. Tarlyon had parked his car outside Claridge's, and thither we walked.

Now Brook Street at that hour is undecided between a state of coma and one of glittering abandon; which means that the deathly silence is every now and then shattered by rich automobiles hurling themselves and lovely ladies all covered in pearls and chrysoprase into the bosom of Grosvenor Square. Claridge's, of course, hath music, so that youth may dance. But of pedestrians along Brook Street there are less than a few . . . and of young men in gents' evening wear running furiously after limousines there is a noticeable scarcity. He simply tore past us, that young man, in the middle of the road, a few yards behind a swiftly-going car. The car stopped towards Grosvenor Square, and somehow the young man seemed to disappear. We were more than fifty yards away, and could not determine whether it was a man or a woman who emerged from the car and entered the house, but it looked like a fat little man. Then the car slid away. The pursuing young man had disappeared.

"He can't have been doing it for fun," said Tarlyon.

"Perhaps he's gone to have a bath," I suggested. For it was a very warm night, and running after motor-cars must have been a wet business.

"We'll see," said Tarlyon. We retraced our steps up Brook Street, and passed the house into which the occupant of the car had disappeared. It was a house like another, dark and silent; and as it stood almost at the corner we went round the corner into Grosvenor Square; at least, we were rounding the corner when a young man in a great hurry collided into us.

"Ah!" said Tarlyon.

"Sorry," said the stranger. I was right about the running—it had made his face very wet.

"So it's you!" said Tarlyon.

"Good-evening, gentlemen," said the Armenian, with a sort of furious courtesy. "If you will excuse me, I am in a hurry." He made to pass us.

"We noticed it," said Tarlyon. "In fact, we noticed nothing else."

"Damn!" snapped the Armenian. "So you saw me running?"

"So did he," I murmured, looking up Brook Street. A policeman was sauntering towards us.

"If you don't want to be asked any questions by the arm of the law," Tarlyon suggested, "you had better take a turn round the square with us."

"I won't move," the stranger muttered passionately. "I have found him at last—I won't move."

"But neither will he," I soothed him. "He's gone into the house. . . ."

"Did you see him go in?"

We nodded.

"Ah, but His Excellency is clever!" said the Armenian viciously.

We grabbed hold of him and hauled him round the square.

"Now," said Tarlyon, "what's all this Excellency nonsense?"

"*He* doesn't think it's nonsense," the young man muttered grimly.

"Look here," I said, "either this is a plot or it is not a plot. In either case you'll look rather an idiot, so—"

"You'd better confide in us," Tarlyon finished. "We, being English, have great sympathy with oppressed peoples—"

"I have noticed it," said the Armenian grimly. He was obviously a well-educated young man.

We had him walking between us, and he never even pretended that he liked our company.

"I suppose," said Tarlyon cattishly, "you've got bombs all over you."

"Sir!" snapped the Armenian.

"Sir to you," said Tarlyon.

"I was merely going to say," said the Armenian, "that in my opinion you are a fool. Do I look the kind of man to carry bombs? I favour the revolver."

"Oh, do you?" said I. Sarcastic I was, you understand.

He looked at me with those large, devilish eyes.

"And one shot," he said gently, "is always enough. . . ."

I gave up.

"And where," asked Tarlyon reasonably, "does His Excellency come in?"

"He won't come in anywhere after to-night. His Excellency is going to die." And with that the Armenian suddenly stopped in his unwilling stride, and looked from one to the other of us. His broken nose made fantasy of his dark face, but I remember thinking that it must once have been a handsome enough face of its kind, for not even a broken nose made him quite ugly. He was as tall as Tarlyon, but slighter; his was a dangerous thinness. He addressed Tarlyon. He did not seem to have a very high opinion of me.

"Sir," he said—an Armenian habit, I suppose, that "sir"— "you have intruded your company on me, but I have accepted you. I have trusted you. I have treated you as gentlemen, being by nature an optimist, and I take it for granted that you will neither betray me nor try to deter me. You will understand the vigour of my purpose when I say that a young girl is concerned in this, that I have sworn a vow, and that if you were in my position you would do what I am going to do. Good-night, gentlemen. I hope we will meet again when I am less occupied with more important business."

"Hold on," cried Tarlyon. "What on earth were you chasing that car for? And who the devil is His Excellency? We'd like to know, you see, so as to be able to pick him out from among the other murders in to-morrow's papers."

"Achmed Jzzit Pasha, the Young Turk," said the Armenian softly.

"Ah!" said George Tarlyon. "I see. Enver Pasha, Djemal Pasha, Talaat Pasha, and Achmed Jzzit Pasha, of the Committee of Union and Progress. I see. Talaat Pasha has already been killed, hasn't he?"

"Four of us," said the Armenian sombrely, "set out from Armenia last year, and each of us had a mission of revenge. One of us—you will remember?—shot and killed Talaat Pasha in a street in Berlin some months ago. Djemal Pasha was lately slain in Syria. Enver Pasha has fled to Bokhara. A murder has been arranged, and will shortly take place in Bokhara. And I, the fourth, have at last found Achmed Jzzit, the foulest murderer of all. There is not an Armenian in the world who would not shoot Achmed Jzzit Pasha on sight if he had the chance—but Armenians who come to Western countries only too soon acquire nasty Western habits of money-grubbing and forget the glory there is in killing. But I, a Zeytounli, have never forgotten it. . . ."

"You speak English very well," I remarked. "Were you educated at an English public-school?"

"That, sir, is a matter of opinion. But even an English public-school could not make me forget that I am an Armenian, and that an Armenian's first business is to kill Turks; failing Turks, he may, of course, kill Kurds or ravish Circassian maidens—"

"Oh, not Circassians!" I pleaded.

"Well, Albanian," he allowed. "During the war I fought through the siege of Zeytoun, and then as an irregular under

Andranik; and since the war I have pursued Achmed Jzzit Pasha—and to-night I have found him! He has been here in London for some months, but under an assumed name, for he knows that he is marked by the Dashnakists[1] and the Henchakists,[1] and he is afraid. It is my present business to cure him of his fear for ever." And with a wrench his arms were free of our gently restraining hands and he was off down the square. But Tarlyon was swift, very swift; I panted up just as he was again "intruding himself" on the Armenian.

"You don't seem to realise," breathed Tarlyon, "that you can't enter a house in Brook Street, kill a Pasha, and get away—"

"I don't care if I get away or not," the other broke in fiercely. "Besides, my friend who killed Talaat in Berlin was acquitted. And I cannot believe that your English juries are as thickheaded as you would have me think. So will you please excuse me, sir?"

It was marvellous what venom that brokennosed young man could put into a simple question!

"I've taken rather a fancy to you," murmured Tarlyon, "and I hate to think of your going off murdering Pashas. Come and have a drink instead, there's a good fellow."

"If I tell you," snapped the Armenian, "that there is a girl in that house, and that I must rescue that girl, then you will perhaps see your way to minding your own business."

"Has the Pasha got your girl?" I asked kindly.

"She is my sister, O fool," he said wearily. "And do you think I can allow my little sister to stay in that loathsome old creature's house one night more than I can help?"

"Collar him," said Tarlyon to me; and I grabbed the young man's other arm, though I didn't in the least want to, and again we began hauling him round the square. As I walked close to

---

[1] Armenian Revolutionary Societies.

him I could feel a solid bulky thing in his hip-pocket, and I did not like the feeling.

"Now," said Tarlyon, very business-like, "what's all this about your sister?"

The Armenian almost screamed with impatience.

"Have I not told you all along that if you were in my position you would do exactly what I am going to do? Must I explain to you that my little sister was carried away by that old lecher before my eyes? Must I tell you how Zeytoun on the hill was at last shelled to dust by the batteries of two Army Corps under Achmed Jzzit Pasha, and how the Turks entered the smoking town and gave no quarter to man, woman or child? Must I, just to satisfy your wanton and asinine curiosity, ravage my heart with retailing how my father and mother were bayoneted before my eyes, and how I escaped only because those Turkish swine thought me already dead? Must I tell you how my little sister was carried away to the harem of Achmed Jzzit Pasha, who, on beholding her, swore a mighty swear that he would not rest from disembowelling Christians until he had ravished her? Did she give way? The slaying went on, day by day and night by night, so that a count of the leaves of the trees in your puny but not unattractive Green Park would make but a fraction of the number of the dead bodies that to this day lie rotting in the plain of Mush. An expert killer was Achmed Jzzit Pasha; and whether or not the natural blood-lust of the illiterate Osmanli was heightened by his oath to ravish my sister I do not know, but I do know that there has not been such a tale of dead Christians since Timur passed through the land to meet Bajazet. And that is the man who holds my sister in that house, while you detain me here with the vain questions and idiotic comments peculiar to the high-minded people of your patrician land. I followed him to Paris, but he escaped me. I found him in Bournemouth, but again I withheld my hand while I planned some way of rescuing Anaïs—fool that

I was! But the idea in my head was that I must first get the girl to some place of safety—and then to come back, slay him, and pay whatever is the penalty in your country for killing a loathsome animal. But now I have realised that there is no other way of rescuing Anaïs but by killing him first. Always, wherever he goes, he keeps her locked in a room next to his, and thus it must be in this house. Bestial fancies seethe in his brain, wherefore he sleeps lightly. And while the night is dwindling, here I stand satisfying your idle curiosity. You really must excuse me now, gentlemen."

"But hold on!" cried Tarlyon. "Why kill the wretched man at all? Why not rescue your sister with the charming name and let the Pasha go on being a Pasha until he dies a horrible death by reason of those bestial fancies which you mentioned? He won't dare come after her—and I don't see much point in getting your sister back if you have got to swing for it more or less at once. Eh, Ralph?"

"Quite right," said I. "Come and have a drink instead."

"This is no time for drink," snapped the Armenian. "The night is dwindling—and how can I desist from killing him when, as I have told you, I cannot get into her room without awaking him? And it stands to reason that as soon as I see him I shall also see red, and kill—as I must, by reason of my vow and by order of the Dashnakists. As I have told you, I would have preferred to have got Anaïs out of the house first, but that seems impossible. . . ."

Tarlyon opened his mouth, and closed it. I knew what was passing in Tarlyon's mind, and I thought I would let it pass, so that he might think again. But then he re-opened his mouth, and this is what he said:

"My friend and I," he said, "might perhaps consider giving you a little assistance, if in return you gave us a promise—"

"I promise nothing!"

"Drat the boy!" said Tarlyon. "What I wish to point out is that, if my friend and I help you to get your sister out of that house, you must drop this killing business. We will contrive some way of keeping His Excellency quiet while you rescue your sister—but you must give us your word of honour, or some efficient substitute, that you will not come back and murder the wretched Pasha. Now, I want no back-chat about it—either you will or you will not."

"But I am bound to the Dashnakists!" cried the Armenian; rather regretfully, I thought.

"Blast the Dashnakists!" said Tarlyon. "Yes or no?"

"I promise," said the Armenian suddenly.

My native common sense now got the better of me.

"You seem to take it for granted that we just walk into the house. How do we get in?"

"This cuts windows like a knife," said the Armenian, showing us in the palm of his hand a glittering little thing like a toy dagger. "An Argentine invention."

"The matter will be further facilitated," said Tarlyon, "by our first getting my car, which is opposite Claridge's, and driving in it to the front door. My reason for this step is that no policeman would dare suspect anything wrong in a house while a Rolls-Royce is standing outside it. Especially, Ralph, when your manly appearance is decorating the driving-seat. . . ."

"I shall be in the house," I said firmly. Not that I wanted to be—but one always says those things, and one always says them firmly.

"Perhaps that would be better," said the Armenian. "It will certainly take the two of you to keep His Excellency quiet while I break in the first locked door I see and get Anaïs. And a RollsRoyce car is, I understand, even more impressive empty than when some one is in it—people make it seem possible."

### III

We got the car and drove bravely to the house. We passed two policemen at the corner of Davies Street, but they were not interested in us. I must say burglary is easy when one has a large and rich car to do it from. . . .

Like all Mayfair houses, this had a tradesmen's entrance; through a little gate on the right of the few steps to the front door, down some steps, and into a little area where was the kitchen door and a window.

"Wait in the car," said the dark young man, and vanished down to the area. We heard a very faint scratching, one little wicked word, a little more scratching; and then the lights blazed up through the glass above the front door, and it was opened. The Armenian stood in the lighted doorway as though he owned the house. I admired him.

Tarlyon's first words when we were in the hall of the house were: "Give me your gun, you charming atrocity."

The Armenian surrendered his revolver without a word; he only sighed. Then he marshalled us.

"Very quiet," he whispered. "And very quick. We must try the upstairs rooms, to see which is his bedroom. One touch on the door will wake him, so you must muffle him at once, else he will rouse the servants. In the meanwhile I will find my sister; then I will take her straight out of the house, and we will await you in the car. I will blow your horn twice, to show that I am awaiting you. It will be kind of you, then, to drive us to Mr. Ritz's hotel in Piccadilly, where, perhaps, with your influence, we may get my sister a lodging for the night. But, remember, keep a tight hold on Achmed Jzzit until I blow the horn—muffle him straightway and let him not open his mouth, else he will bring the whole neighbourhood down on us. Let us begin."

We began with a bit of luck—or so it seemed. Having tiptoed up to the first landing, the very first door we touched held the lightly-sleeping Pasha. We knew he was there by the howl that followed our touching the door-knob—indeed, he was a light sleeper, that man of bestial fancies! But we gave him no time to make a real noise; we leapt into the room; I switched on the light, Tarlyon leapt on bed and Pasha, I leapt after Tarlyon, and in a second we held him, making smothered howling noises under the bedclothes. We had not even had time to see if he was young or old, but the shape of him suggested that he was older than most people. His was, however, an active and restless shape. We were very gentle with him, almost too gentle, for once a distinct howl issued from somewhere under the sheets.

"Steady," said George Tarlyon to the restless shape.

"You'll throttle yourself," said George Tarlyon.

To prevent him from doing that we, with a sudden and well-concerted movement, unscrewed his head and muffled him with a handkerchief. We looked upon his face for the first time.

"You're a nasty, cruel old man," said George Tarlyon.

Achmed Jzzit Pasha looked all that the Armenian had said he was, and more. A fierce old face it was that looked murder at us. His eyes, under white, bushy eyebrows, were frantic and furious, and never for a second did he cease to struggle. I thought of that fine old Turkish warrior of the last century, the man of Plevna, Osman Pasha; this old man is of the same breed, I thought.

We had so far heard nothing of the Armenian; but that Achmed Jzzit Pasha realised that we two were only accessories was evident, for not even his struggling with us concealed the fact that he was listening, listening intently.

A slight noise, as of a drawer hastily banged, came from the next room. It was only a small noise, but it had a mighty effect on the old slayer of men. His eyes simply tore at us, his fat little body heaved frantically, he bit my finger in trying to howl—he went quite mad, that violent old Turk. I admonished him severely:

"It's only little Anaïs packing up to go away with her brother," I told him; but that old Turk knew not resignation nor repentance, and still we had gently to battle with him.

"He's an infernally long time about it," grumbled Tarlyon at last—and at that very moment the horn outside blew twice. We welcomed it.

"Now," said Tarlyon to the heaving old man, "we are about to release you. Your girl has flown, so it's too late for you to make a noise. So don't." And for form's sake he showed the revolver, though I never saw a man who looked less likely to use it. "You may not realise it," he added severely, "but we have saved your life. After the first shock has worn off you will thank two disinterested men for having saved you from the wrath of an Armenian."

With another sudden and well-concerted movement we let go. The Pasha did not make a noise. It was evident he realised that it was too late to make a noise. But in the next few seconds he revealed, for a Turk, an astonishing knowledge of the baser words and idioms of the English language. Then he leapt out of bed, a funny little creature in pink flannel pyjamas, and rushed out of the room. Breathless, we found him in the next room.

Now I have very little acquaintance with girls' bedrooms, but a glance was sufficient to show me that no girl alive could have a bedroom like that. There was no bed in it, and very little else; just a thing like a tallboy, but made of steel, or so it looked: and that, if I may say so, had certainly been ravished. . . .

Then the old man really began to howl, and we hadn't the heart to stop him. He howled himself back to the bedroom, and we followed him, looking and feeling like all the things he said we were.

"But aren't you Achmed Jzzit Pasha?" I pleaded. But the life had suddenly gone out of him; he sat on the edge of the bed.

"My name is Wagstaffe," he said weakly, "and I have the finest collection of Roman coins in the country. Or rather, I had. My son, Michael Wagstaffe, has them now—thanks to you two idiots!"

Tarlyon had an idea which took him to the window; I had the same idea, and followed him. We looked down upon the face of Brook Street, and behold! it was empty. Never was a

Rolls-Royce car with lamps alight so invisible. We went back to Mr. Wagstaffe on the edge of the bed.

"We are sorry," I muttered, but he seemed not to hear us. George Tarlyon is usually a fine upstanding fellow, and some people have thought him handsome, but now he looked as though he had seen horrid spectres after dining entirely on *pâté de foie gras*.

Mr. Wagstaffe was whispering, almost to himself: "Two years ago, when I drove him out of the house, he swore that one day he would steal my coins. And now he has stolen my coins. I always knew he would keep his word, for he is a devil. And he always knew that, come what might, I would not prosecute my son for a thief . . . My Roman coins!" And Mr. Wagstaffe wept.

We explained our position to him. We gave him a brief outline of the facts. We begged him to understand. We pointed out that if his son really had been an Armenian and if he had really been Achmed Jzzit Pasha we had undoubtedly saved his life. I couldn't help thinking that he ought to be grateful to us, but I didn't say that.

He seemed to find a little solace in our discomfiture.

"Ah, he's a clever boy, Michael," sighed Mr. Wagstaffe. "He is always on the look-out for what he calls the Mugs. I gather that you two gentlemen are Mugs—the same, perhaps, as what are known in America as Guys. But I, his father, can assure you that he is not an Armenian; nor has he ever been nearer to Armenia than the Bankruptcy Court, but he has been there twice. He calls himself the cavalier of the streets, but when he is up to any of his tricks he disguises himself as an Armenian—the disguise consisting merely of his saying he is an Armenian. It's so simple, he says, for the Mugs believe him at once, on the ground that no one would say he was an Armenian if he wasn't. I have only been back from America a week, and he must have been searching all London for me. He probably saw me at the theatre this evening, and was going to raid my house alone when you two intelligent gentlemen got in his way. But he is not a bad boy really—he's got ideas, that's what it is; and also Mugs have an irresistible fascination for him. Take your case, for instance. I have no doubt but that he will be ready to return me my coins in exchange for a cheque—though, of course, that depends on the cheque. And I can see, gentlemen, that you are eager to show your regret for breaking into my house and assaulting my person by offering to pay the cheque yourselves. I thank you; though, indeed, it is the least you can do, and an infinitely more convenient way of settling the matter than wearisome arguments in a police-court—provided, of course, that house-breaking and assault are matters for argument. I have never yet heard they were. . . ."

I giggled. I simply couldn't help it.

"That's all very well," said Tarlyon, "but what about my car?"

"What is the matter with your car?" asked Mr. Wagstaffe gently.

"There's so damn little the matter with it," snapped Tarlyon, "that it's probably half-way down the Dover road by now."

"Ah," said Mr. Wagstaffe wearily. "I see. Cars have an irresistible fascination for Michael. I see. I am sorry. Was it a good car?"

"Pity," said Mr. Wagstaffe. "A great pity. He may, of course, return it. He may. You cannot, of course, compel him to, for it would be difficult for you, in your position, to put the police on him. But he may return it on his own. Michael is not a bad boy, really. He will, I am sure, communicate with me as to what I will offer for the return of my coins. I will then give him the cheque you have so kindly promised to post to me to-night, and perhaps he will soften also as regards your car and return it to you. Naturally, he will expect your cheque to approximate to the value of your car—say, half its value. Michael is something of an expert about the value of cars. That's why I said it was a pity, sir, a pity that your car was not a cheap car. But I am sure you will have no difficulty in finding a taxi-cab home. They are so abundant in Grosvenor Square that my sleep is often disturbed by them. . . ."

The rest of the story is not at all interesting. George Tarlyon's car was finally returned, and George Tarlyon is sorry that Mr. Michael Wagstaffe's nose is already broken.

# The Luck of Captain Fortune

Now it happened that one night, not long ago, Shelmerdene, having nothing better to do, rang me up and, complaining thus and thus, suggested that I should do the manly thing and dine with her. It was such a rare happening that I remember it all vividly. I remember I adopted an offended attitude, asking her if she thought I was the kind of man who was so lacking in dinner engagements that I could be rung up to take a lady out to dinner at the last moment. I asked her who she thought I was. I asked her to dine at the Ritz. But then, after a certain amount of talk this way and that way, we decided that we would be frightfully gay, and so we went to dine at the Ambassadors.

Of course, you know the Ambassadors. Every one knows the Ambassadors. Every one has passed through its mean but patrician-looking entrance in Bond Street, just between a jeweller's and a fishmonger's. It is, of course, a Night-Club, though there is nothing to prevent you going there in the afternoon if you feel that way. It is an exclusive Night-Club. Outside it are posted tall men in brilliant uniforms adorned with medals, and these men have the eyes of hawks, for it is their business to sift out the low and vulgar from the fashionable crowds that perpetually strive for admittance; they are the best sifters of their kind; and on any night of the week you will see at the Ambassadors all the quality and only the quality, toying with their food and calling each other by their Christian names.

The tables are elegantly arranged around the walls, deep sofas and divans are luxuriously set about them, while the centre is left unchallenged to the shimmering parquet floor. Of course all parquet floors shimmer, but none shimmers like this at the Ambassadors. One dines. One sups. Tommy Tittlebat's Saxophone Six plays. The quality dance. The more Tommy Tittlebat's Saxophone Six plays the more the quality dance, which is only reasonable. They jump up to dance at the exact moment when their food is put upon the table, and they cease dancing only when their food has become so cold that they have to hold lighted matches under the plates to warm them up. This causes much laughter.

As evening melts exquisitely into night, the quality enter the Ambassadors in their hundreds, all calling each other and the waiters by their Christian names. Some bring well-dressed nobodies with them, some bring Jews, some bring titled what-nots from the provinces or from Labrador: so that by midnight the parquet floor is so crowded that you cannot see the parquet. Then it is great fun to dance.

The game is played like this. As soon as a man and woman, sitting at their table, see a clear square foot of parquet floor they instantly leap on same, and, passionately embracing each other thereon, make movements of their eyebrows, hips, and feet in time to Tommy Tittlebat's Saxophone Six. That is called dancing. They stay on their square foot of shimmering parquet floor until they get shoved off it by a beefier couple, whereupon the two gentlemen compliment each other in an elegant way—as is the way with persons of *ton*—or they call each other names (not Christian names)—as is also the way with persons of *ton*—until one or other of them is thrown out. That is called enjoying yourself, and you have to pay to do it. I paid, on the night I am telling you about. But not even Tommy Tittlebat's Saxophone Six could drown the charm of Shelmerdene. Dear Shelmerdene. . . .

At the table next to us sat a solitary gentleman. Obviously, we thought, he is waiting for some one, and obviously that some one has let him down. I am not much of a connoisseur as to men's looks, but Shelmerdene knows about these things, and she said he was handsome. He was, even as he sat, noticeably tall; of strong and manly appearance; and, though swarthy in countenance, so essentially English-looking that it was with a disagreeable shock that, towards midnight, we noticed that his dark eyes were wet with tears. There is, as a rule, a scarcity of six-foot men weeping over supper at the Ambassadors.

"Drunk," I suggested harshly, but Shelmerdene is a kind woman and she said that he looked like a man haunted by a great calamity.

"That's all very well," I said, "but one doesn't cry about things." Whereupon Shelmerdene looked at me, those wide and wise and witty eyes looked full at me—men have drowned themselves in Shelmerdene's eyes—and I saw laughter at all men playing in their dusky-blue depths; and I had to confess to those kind, mocking eyes, that I, Ralph Wyndham Trevor, had also wept, that I had sobbed like a child, and that a woman had seen me at it—the woman who had caused it.

"Exactly," said Shelmerdene. "For the more virile a man is, the braver and the more adventurous a man is, the more likely he is to weep before a woman and generally make a fool of himself. Fetch me that handsome man, Ralph. Men in love are not generally very reticent, especially Englishmen in love. The reticence of Englishmen is as much an illusion as the good manners of Frenchmen. I am curious. Fetch me that handsome man, Ralph."

I leant over to the table beside us. The tall, dark young man turned moist, absent-minded eyes upon me.

"Sir," I said, "forgive this unpardonable intrusion. But my companion and I have observed your solitude, no doubt temporary, and would be delighted if you would join us in a glass of wine."

"You are very kind," said the tall, dark young man.

He refused, with a courtly gesture, to take my seat on the sofa beside Shelmerdene, but sat on a chair opposite us. I filled him a glass of champagne.

"Sir," said he, "your health. And yours, madam."

But still the tears did not leave those dark, tragic eyes, they smouldered darkly in them. He looked infinitely wretched, though he bravely tried to smile as he addressed Shelmerdene:

"You must not think me unamiable if I do not ask you to dance, but I am not, to-night, in my happiest vein. You must forgive me. . . ."

He looked so very miserable that I was about to say something sympathetic when Shelmerdene kicked me under the table. She murmured something gentle across the table. . .

"You are so kind and sympathetic," whispered the handsome stranger, "that I will tell you a story. You are sure it won't bore you?"

We said we were quite sure, and I filled him a glass of champagne.

"Sir," said he, "your health. And yours, madam."

"My story," he addressed us, "concerns a man and a woman. The man loved the woman. I call her a woman because all words are vain, and to call her a goddess were but to lay myself under the charge of affectation. But if I were to tell you her name, which of course I cannot do, except to say that it rhymes with custard, you would instantly agree with the most abandoned epithets for her beauty; for she is one of the best loved ladies in the land, by reason of her high birth, her peerless carriage, and her amazing loveliness. I tell you, she has no rival in the present, nor can history tell us of her like. If the Lady Circe had had golden hair, which I much doubt, perhaps she may have been a tithe as lovely. It is, as you know, said of the Lady Circe that she turned men into swine, but this lady turns swine into men, and what could be more agreeable than that? It was ever her innocent delight to improve the men she met; and, with such beauty, was there anything she could not do with men? Her beauty appals the epithet. She is divinely tall, gold is but brass beside the sheen of her hair, and white samite is gray beside her complexion. She is without doubt the loveliest woman in England—which, of course, also includes America, for all lovely American women live in England even though they may die in Paris.

"The man met this lady, and instantly loved her. Now his was no casual passion. She was young, but the war had already widowed her; and she seemed not unaware of, nor entirely repelled by, her new suitor's passion, for from her many suitors she chose him as her constant companion. Thus, rumour very soon came to link their names; and rumour, generally so malignant, was then kind enough to find something harmonious in the alliance of that pair. For he was a man of unusual height, of a good name, a distinguished military record, and looks which some have thought handsome while none have denied to be very properly suited to the requirements of an English gentleman.

"She did not, at first, wholly accept him. But no day passed that they did not meet; and, as day exquisitely strung itself to day so that each was another pearl on the necklace of an Olympian goddess, she seemed, by sudden gestures, by sudden impulses, to be growing to love him—she the loveliest lady in the world! And he was happy—Oh, God, he was happy!"

The handsome stranger fell silent, and I thought he was about to break down. I filled him a glass of champagne.

"Sir," said he, "your health. And yours, madam."

"I have told you," he went on, "of her amazing beauty, the golden-white beauty of the world's last aristocracy. But, as though that were not enough, she was ambitious; she was a lady of parts, and she increasingly sought the company of those with whom she could discuss, deeply and seriously, the current problems of this vexed time. She was, you understand, tremendously interested in improving people; and politically she was, of course, a Die-Hard; for, as the daughter of a great house, her earliest experiences in literature was *The Morning Toast*, to which she had remained faithful even when she grew up, with that tenacity peculiar to all readers of that remarkable journal. And so, when the franchise was extended to women, she, even before Lady Astor, raised the standard of rampant womanhood; and the world was given the rare sensation of seeing, and the House of Commons the rare privilege of welcoming, among its foremost legislators, the loveliest lady in the land, or any land. Words cannot describe the effect she made as she stood, indisputably the first of the twelve other ladies who had won their right of entrance into the Lower House, in all her glorious height and golden beauty among the dolorous decorations of that crypt which the glamour of centuries has raised to the majesty of Britain's greatest institution.

"It was at this time that the man I have referred to came into her life; and it chanced for her to be a fortunate occasion, for without him her political career had been a barren thing. She could not make up a speech. Memorise and speak a speech she could, so amazingly well that the populace cried out with wonder at one so gifted with brains and elocution as well as with beauty—but she could not make up a speech. The brains in her speeches, which were rapidly winning for her a foremost position among the Die-Hards, were not hers. Her friend wrote her speeches for her. He did them gladly, happy and honoured to be of use to her. He 'helped' her with her speeches, so that she seemed not to be aware that his was every idea, every phrase, every epigram, everything—and that was his greatest pleasure, his subtle 'helping' her to a place of honour and esteem for something besides her beauty. Himself, though a gentleman, was not a Die-Hard: he was a man of ideas. He had a brain like Clapham Junction, going this way and that way and every way at the same time; and he could, no doubt, have made a great political name for himself, but he was by nature a soldier and by temperament adventurous, so that it pleased him infinitely more to 'help' the lady of his dreams to political fame rather than to bid for it in his own person.

"But another soldier came into her life—the most fearless soldier of our time, it has been said. But whether it was that he was the most fearless or the luckiest, we cannot tell. He himself insists on his luck. 'I cannot lose,' he is reported to have often said, sometimes unhappily. Whatever he touched became a jewel in his hand: whatever he ventured, he won. A name never expressed a man more perfectly—Victor Fortune! Captain Fortune, V.C., D.S.O., M.C., etc. . . .

"He saw her first from the Strangers' Gallery in the Lower House. He was, of course, familiar with her beauty—how often had he not seen portraits of her in the fashionable journals of the day!—but her face had hitherto failed to attract him, because of a certain coldness, a certain vapidity, which only his fastidious taste has chosen to discover in it. But those were photographs—now, from his obscure seat in the Gallery, Captain Fortune looked down upon the fairest figure the mind of man could conceive.

"It was the afternoon set apart for the discussion on Fabric Gloves, and the loveliest woman of our time excelled herself in her speech: or, rather, her friend had excelled himself. Captain Fortune, gazing down upon that tall and golden figure, a light in that dark pit of legislation, was enthralled and—yes, appalled by her beauty and her wit. It had needed only her wit, her culture, to add that vivacity to her perfect features which would enslave Captain Fortune's fastidious heart—Victor Fortune, who never ventured but he won! He met the lady that night, at Lady Savoury's ball in aid of the Bus-Conductors' Orphanage.

"Three weeks later her old friend, her 'helper,' was stunned to read in *The Morning Toast* of the engagement of the lady to Captain Fortune, V.C., D.S.O., M.C., etc. He was stunned; then, frantically, he rushed to her house. She was not yet fully dressed, she received him with pretty confusion. She was very sorry about it all, she said. She was frightfully sorry, she said. But she had fallen in love. Victor Fortune was so fine, so magnificent—and it needed but her love and care to help him combat his few weaknesses, which might be counted human in other men but were unworthy and degrading in such a man as Victor Fortune.

"And so he went away, her friend, never to return. He never has returned. He never will return, for thus it is written. And Captain Fortune, who never ventured but he won, married his lady, the lady of his dreams. . . ."

What could we say? We could only say that we were very sorry, frightfully sorry, but his lovely lady had already told him that and it did not seem to have soothed him. Tears smouldered in those dark eyes, and I thought he was going to break down. I filled him a glass of champagne.

"Sir," said he, "your health. And yours, madam."

"Of course," he whispered, "she has never been able to make a speech since. How could she? Without her old friend she is just a lovely woman, a lovely woman whose life centres round her care for Captain Fortune. And her old friend has gone out of her life, he who loved her and still loves her, never to return, never. . . ."

He rose from his chair and looked miserably down on us. Bravely, he tried to smile.

"I am so, so sorry," murmured Shelmerdene.

And silently we watched his tall figure carving a passage through the quality to the doorway. A broken man is a more miserable thing than a broken toy, and we were sad. . . .

The agreeable and polished M. Risotto, prince of *maîtres d'hôtels*, chanced by our table.

"Who," asked Shelmerdene, "was that tall gentleman who has just left us?"

"That, madam," said the agreeable and polished M. Risotto, "is Captain Fortune, the most gallant gentleman in England. . . ."

# The Ancient Sin

## I

George Tarlyon and I were engaged to stay the week-end with Aubrey Carlyle at Malmanor Hall, which is four hours by car from Hyde Park Corner, though that, of course, rather depends on the kind of car. George Tarlyon's—as that Armenian fellow had noticed—was a good car, long and low, a chap's car, and we had run four-fifths of our distance very well: we had flashed through a town, whose name is of no interest, and had plunged into the peculiar wood of Carmion, which shrouds the southern border of the domain of Malmanor. We were therefore on the last lap, and the fact that this lay through Carmion Wood lent a certain interest to it; for although Tarlyon and I had very often stayed with Aubrey Carlyle at Malmanor, we had never, somehow, really penetrated into Carmion. I don't know why, but it just hadn't happened; and George Tarlyon was now running his car along the broad sweep of its central and only road because of a vague idea that it was a short cut as compared to the main road. It was a rotten idea, that of George Tarlyon's.

One of the many silly legends about Carmion Wood is that only foreigners may hear the singing of the birds therein, while for Englishmen there is no sound but the rustling of the leaves and the sighing of the boughs. How that sort of nonsense ever gets hold of a countryside, I don't know. And the fact that, as George Tarlyon rushed the car along the twilight road—for although it was a bright summer's day, the leaves are very thick on Carmion trees—we could hear no birds singing was, without a doubt, simply because they were singing somewhere else that afternoon.

"Obviously," I said to Tarlyon, who had suggested that had I had a Spanish mother I could now be enjoying the sweet trilling of rooks and the back-chat of black-birds, "obviously they can't always be singing in one place."

"Listen," said George Tarlyon, and when you listened it really was rather curious, the silence of Carmion Wood. "Quiet we call silence, the merest word of all," some one has written, Poe, I think; but that word applied very fully to Carmion, it was so silent! If only there had been a wind, just to give the leaves a little fun! But there wasn't a breath, it was a close day in August, and the wood was a crypt, that's what it was. I said so to Tarlyon, but all he said was that he was hungry. Later on he grunted: "You and your crypts!"

"It's a pity," I said reasonably, "that the sun doesn't get a bit further into this place. . . ."

"Dolorous is the word for it," murmured Tarlyon; and he was quite right, amazingly right. "Dolorous" was certainly the word for it.

"Open your cut-out, man!" I said at last, for that car was really too well-bred. And with a twist of his foot he opened the cut-out. What a cut-out! But it did make things seem more homely.

## II

The car rushed on. . . . The straight road under the thick tapestry of leaves would take us directly to the parkland of Malmanor; through the opening at the end, for Carmion Wood ends sharply, we could see in the far distance, lying in the hollow of the county like an ancient pink jewel in a green bowl, the vast Elizabethan pile of Malmanor Hall.

The car rushed on . . .

"Bang!" said the car, but Tarlyon said worse than that as he pulled up.

"This," I said, as we looked at the flattened back tyre, "this comes of taking short cuts." The matter with Tarlyon was that he had no luncheon and was hungry. Now George Tarlyon is my greatest friend, but this I had against him, that he swore too much. Like many other men, decent men, he swore too much and too often. I can say "damn" with any man, I have said "bloody," and will again when it is organic to the occasion, but what humorous writers in the magazines call scientific swearing does not amuse me. I do not wish to seem superior, but it just does not amuse me. In the Middle Ages men swore mightily on the names of the Trinity and the Saints, but then they believed mightily in the Trinity and the Saints. Now men swear and curse on the names of everything and believe in nothing. It is the habit of the modern world; it is the habit of being in a hurry; it is the habit of unholiness. And it had grown on my friend, George Almeric St. George Tarlyon, who was otherwise a reasonable sort of man.

To put on the spare tyre was only the work of a few minutes; and again the car rushed on . . . and from behind us came a cry. I looked back, and there, twenty yards behind us, stood and screamed a woman by the roadway.

Tarlyon was really remarkably fluent as he reversed. He was hungry, you see.

"We must have dropped something," I suggested.

We drew abreast of the gesticulating woman on the coarse grass by the road. She was just a slip of an aged woman, and her hair was made of bits of gray string, and her eyes leapt hysterically out of a little lined face. "Come, come!" she was screaming. "Come, come quick!" She smelt old, that woman.

The car had scarcely stopped abreast of her when she turned and scampered away along a little lane between the tall, still trees. It was extraordinary, the way she ran, that little old woman! "Come, come quick!"

Well, there was nothing to do but to follow.

"The girl's mad," snarled Tarlyon, as he strode after the little old woman. But striding was no use, it was a running job, and it was a hot day.

It was an untidy, tangled path up which she was leading us—and how quickly she ran, that little old woman, stumbling over her uncertain feet and frantic gestures, while we ploughed on behind her through the lush of the wood in July. It was an amazingly hot day; the Press for the last week or so had been full of surprise and congratulation as to the amazingly hot days we were having, and we had now an unrivalled opportunity of testing the veracity of the Press, but we would much rather have forgone it. At that moment, following that little old woman up that tangled path in Carmion Wood, George Tarlyon and I were probably the wettest men in England outside of a swimming-bath.

"What the devil is it all about?" muttered Tarlyon, and was not soothed by my suggesting that I thought it was all part of his idea of a short cut to Malmanor—while the little old woman still screamed at us to come quick, quick.

"Quick, quick . . ." And at her heels we burst out on to a clearing in the wood. The sun lay on that clearing like a carpet of gold.

### III

Tarlyon and I stopped dead, and stared. We stared hard. But the little old woman, still screaming to us to follow, ran on ahead to the house. Yes, there was a house in that clearing, a little farmhouse. And the sun lay on it all like a carpet of gold: that is how I saw it. . . .

"Not our business," muttered Tarlyon, and I heartily agreed that it wasn't. We stood where we were, with our eyes glued on what we saw; and George Tarlyon dug his hands deep in his pockets. George Tarlyon always dug his hands deep in his pockets when the wanted frightfully to take them out.

A man was thrashing his son. I cannot explain why, but we were somehow quite certain that the thing the man was thrashing was flesh of his flesh and blood of his blood. He was a huge man, with a mane of gray hair and a long gray beard, and he had on a bright red shirt. If I close my eyes now I can see the blood-red of that huge bearded man's shirt, I can see the curve of his great shoulders and the muscles that stood out like lumps of rubber on his half-bare arm as he beat his son with a stout stick. And I can see his little old wife trying to stay his hand, begging, praying, moaning. We heard her moaning, like an old, old bird in pain. And at that Tarlyon started forward a step. . . .

"Steady there!" cried Tarlyon sharply. "Steady, Beaver!" The cry cut across the sunlit place, the clear cry that has lit for England the darkest corners of the world, and the huge man in the red shirt stayed his cudgel and looked at us. But the little old woman still moaned, and it was quite dreadful to hear that in the summer silence. Ten yards separated us from that domestic scene, but they were yards of bright sunlight, and we could see every line on that patriarch's face. For he was a patriarch. He was the most magnificent man I have ever seen; and Tarlyon and I, not small men, felt withered under his straight look. We stood rooted.

"Friends," said the old man, and his was the voice of authority, "you must leave me in peace to drive the sin out of this my son. His mother is a woman, and will pardon everything in those she loves, but you are men and know the one sin that is unpardonable by all men. Go your ways in peace, and fear not to put your own houses in order. . . ."

And still he looked at us, that remarkable old lecturer, his cudgel stayed in the air, his son at his feet; and his voice was the voice of a man who has drunk the vinegar of life, and his eyes were the eyes of a man who has seen Christ crucified. That is why we knew for certain, Tarlyon and I, that whatever that ancient man said was true, and whatever he did was right. "Come away," I whispered.

"You are right. It is your business," cried Tarlyon across the sunlight—and, dear God, it was! For the thing happened then. We hadn't noticed that the son had crawled from his father's feet. And what we saw was a spade raised high in the sunlight, a spade crashing down and cleaving the patriarch's head like an axe, so that the blood came out of it like the sap of a tight orange. Without a cry the old man fell, and red as his shirt were the stones of the yard beneath his head. The little old woman screamed. The son and his spade lay where Tarlyon's right hand felled him, and Tarlyon knelt by the slaughtered old man. I couldn't move. I took up the gored spade and held it, a silly gesture. My heart beat like a bell in my ears, and I remember there rose to my lips prayers that I thought I had forgotten.

"Quiet, for one moment," I heard Tarlyon's voice to the screaming old woman. I stared and wondered at my friend, kneeling there on the dyed stones and listening to the heart under the red shirt. I could not have done that. I hate a lot of blood.

Then he rose and came towards me. I hated the dark damp patches on his trouser-knees.

"Quite dead," he said. "We must fetch the police."

Of course, I thought. And together we looked down at the son on the ground. He was gibbering. He had gone mad. "Drat the boy!" said Tarlyon thoughtfully.

"I wonder," I heard myself whisper, "what was the one sin the old man said was unpardonable?"

Tarlyon looked from the prostrate thing to me, and I saw that those slightly frozen blue eyes of his were as miserable as the eyes of a hurt girl. You see, that old man was a very remarkable old man, and he was dead. . . .

"I don't know," he whispered back. "You and I, Ralph, and our friends, have become so civilised that we don't know what the unpardonable sins are. We simply don't *know*, old man! We are the world's soft people, Ralph. We are so civilised that we pardon too much—both in ourselves and other people; and we call that being broad minded, but it's really being flabby. But that old man, I'm sure, was not 'broad-minded,' he was as little 'broad-minded' as Jehovah, and there was one sin he simply would not pardon. And we, who are civilised people, do not even know what it was. . . ."

We stared silently at the poor gibbering thing at our feet.

"Better tie him up before leaving," I suggested.

"Don't you think," said Tarlyon, "that one of us should stay here while—"

"I won't stay here alone," I said abruptly—and I meant it. Nothing would have induced me to stay alone in that ghastly sunlit spot, alone with that lunatic boy and the little old woman and the butchered patriarch. How she moaned, that little old woman kneeling on the blooded stones. . . .

With a silk handkerchief for his ankles and one for his wrists, we trussed the poor boy against the kitchen door. He could not have been more than seventeen or so, and his young face was hideous with fear.

We left the place quickly; but I looked back just once at the scene, for it seemed to me very strange of the sun still to lie on it all like a carpet of gold. That is how I felt about it.

## IV

Swiftly Tarlyon put the bonnet of his car to the direction from which we had come, where lay the town whose name is of no interest.

"How far is it, d'you think, Ralph?"

"About four miles," I ventured; and Tarlyon proceeded to eat up those four miles as a conjuror eats up yards of ribbon. It perished beneath us, that road, and the roaring cut-out tore the silence of Carmion Wood into a million bits, and may it never have found them again! Neither of us spoke. I was feeling sick.

We reached the outskirts of the town, and a piece of luck saved us from inquiring for the police station; for, approaching us on a bicycle, we saw a blue, helmeted figure, and by the stripes on his arm we knew him for a sergeant of police. Tarlyon pulled up.

"Better leave the bicycle and come with us to Carmion Wood," he said. "Explain as we go. Urgent."

The sergeant looked closely into Tarlyon's face.

"Right, sir," said he, and quickly gave the custody of his bicycle to a gnarled-looking woman in the open doorway of a labourer's dwelling.

"What's oop over ut Carmion?" asked she.

"You may well ask," said Tarlyon.

No laggard was that sergeant of police. A grizzled man, with a reticent face. I sat behind and heard Tarlyon explain. The sergeant said nothing, listening intently, until the end.

"Where did you say the house was, sir?" he asked then.

"I've just been telling you, man! In a little clearing in the wood."

"Very good, sir," said the sergeant of police.

Silently we sped into Carmion Wood.

"You see, sir," said the sergeant, "it's a powerful long time since I've been here. Folk roundabout mislike the wood."

"Don't feel very attached to it myself," grunted Tarlyon. "Ah, here we are!"

But it was not going to be as easy as that. For when we left the car, at the identical spot where, we were certain, the little old woman had stopped us, we somehow lost our way. We wandered about for some time, up little twisting lanes, down tangled untidy lanes, up no lanes at all: we ploughed through the growth and lush of the wood, like angry flies beating about a crypt to which the sun filtered in tortured patches of light. We perspired enormously—and Tarlyon lost his temper. He had had no luncheon, you understand, and it was now past five; and so he was fluent in the forbidden language. But the sergeant of police was a tough and silent man, he neither sweated nor spoke.

"Where did you say the house was, sir?" asked the sergeant at last: and very amiably, I thought, considering. . . .

"Oh," says Tarlyon. "So you've heard me mention a house, have you!"

We stood very still, the three of us, and Tarlyon glared.

"Look here, sergeant," he snarled, "if you ask me again where that house is I shall get cross . . . I've told you, man! Body of God, if—"

"*Please*, sir!" said the sergeant quickly.

"What d'you mean by 'Please, sir?'" Tarlyon was well away. It was a very warm day, you understand.

"I mean, sir," said the sergeant of police, "please don't swear on the name or the body of God."

## V

Well, we went on . . . and, at last, unmistakably hit the path up which we had followed the little old woman. We followed the path, Tarlyon first, then me, then the sergeant. And then we came upon the clearing, and the sun lay on it like a carpet of gold. We stared. Like idiots, we stared. For, except the sun, there was nothing in that clearing but the rust and bones of a long-ruined house.

You had, of course, suspected as much. You had known that all along. You know all about those silent woods and slaughtered men. You have been let in before, by better men. But it was curious, all the same. . . .

"Is this where you said the house was, sir?" the sergeant's voice came gently.

We turned and looked at him.

"Because," he went on, "there's been no house here for more than thirty year. . . ."

"Ah!" said Tarlyon; that was about as much as any one *could* say. And our eyes wandered over the clearing, and we saw, bright against the mouldy stones of the ruin, two silk handkerchiefs. . . .

Even the law was at last affected by the heat, for he raised his helmet and passed a hand over his almost bald head.

"Yes," said the sergeant of police. "There was a house here thirty year ago, but it was burnt down by the men of the neighbourhood because of a great crime that was done there. Patricide it was, but the boy was pardoned, being judged mad, and mad he must have been to kill the best and most God-fearing man in the county. Good-day, sirs. I'll walk my way back. Yours was just an illusion, I make no doubt. The sun, maybe. But it's always had a bad name, has Carmion . . . Good-day, sirs." And the sergeant of police went his way.

"Did you see him, did you see his face?" I gasped frantically. For the face of the sergeant of police was the grown face of the lunatic boy we had trussed up an hour before with our two silk handkerchiefs, and they lying where we must have dropped them, drooping over the ruins. . . .

"And he has learnt his lesson," said Tarlyon, and his face was as still as the gray water of a rock-pool. "He has learnt his lesson, Ralph—and has taught me one. For the one sin that the old man said was unpardonable by all men is blasphemy. . . ."

# The Cavalier of the Streets

## I

It would not have occurred to you that Mrs. Avalon was a discontented woman. It would not even have occurred to you that she could be, for what had she not? She was, of course, the wife of John Avalon, K.C. But she was more than that, she was Fay Avalon. Now of the lovely, the gracious Fay Avalon, what shall be said that has not already been said? She was a figure of the world, and in it most centrally situated. She had not pushed, but she was *there*. More, she was a figure of legend, remote and courteous. Every one knew about her, but of nothing against her, and this was so because she was a lady who never by any means sought any publicity but that which the love and respect of her wide acquaintance spread for her. She was, in fact, a darling. It was the fashion to speak well of Fay Avalon, and it is only shallow people who say that all fashions are shallow because they change. There is nothing in the world that does not change, and if fashions change oftener than most that is because—well, it is difficult to say exactly why that is, and anyway this is not the place for it.

Now why are people like sheep? But perhaps it would be better to ask: "Why, in nearly all novels and conversations, is there one law for the rich and another for the poor?" For in nearly all novels and conversations there is a sort of asinine implication that among the rich, the social, there is no real friendship, but that real friendship exists only among the poor. For years and years and years England has been living under a tyranny, a silly tyranny: it is called the middle-class, and it is belauded by all because nearly all belong to it. Now if a writer writes of the middle-class he is said to have a sense of the Reality of Life, but if he writes of the poor wretches who continue to eke out a miserable existence on their capital in Mayfair, it is said of him that he is writing of people who do not matter, people who are not worth writing about, people among whom none of the real emotions exist, and so on. The patricians never protest, for a gentleman is one who can take abuse properly, the same, of course, applying to a lady. But the others, the Backbone of England! Oh, what a Backbone that is, and how swiftly it becomes a jawbone when it is scratched by a well-aimed bit of contumely! But what does all that matter, particularly when we were talking of Fay Avalon, and how charming she was. She had many real friends, and these confided much in her, but in them she did not confide. Fay Avalon was not capable of telling even the least of her troubles to any one, for she was shy. Beneath her polish, her wit, her grave courtesy—a rare enchantment, that—her supreme ability as a hostess at whose table enemies were notably changed to friends, she was as shy as a girl. Never, never, in all her brilliant life, and it really was a very brilliant life, had she been able to exclude the idea that she might very easily bore people, that, in fact, she was not nearly so clever and amusing as other people. That is why she never confided: she only seemed to. . . .

One of the many secrets that Fay Avalon hid within herself was that she was romantic, deeply. She had always been romantic. John Avalon, K.C. had never been romantic, and never knew anything of his wife's trouble. He loved his wife jealously, but being a great K.C. is, of course, a very tiring way of life, and so he spent most of his time with her in sleeping.

Romance came into the life of Fay Avalon at a time when she would sometimes say: "I am older than most women." She was thirty-eight years old, and so she was sorry for herself, and then romance came. It was Prince Nicholas Pavlovitch Shuvarov who brought it. He was, of course, a refugee from Bolshevy, and it was said that before the Revolution his people had owned half of Petrograd, as was only natural, for there are countless Russians of the old order in London and Paris whose people once owned halves of Petrograd, not to speak of the Grand Dukes who made such a mess of all of it. But Prince N. P. Shuvarov was charming, and he was an artist. You knew that because people went about saying he was charming and an artist. You were asked to respect him because he earned his living, and of course you did what you were asked, although you were not aware of any particular esteem instantly alight in the eyes of those to whom you volunteered the information that you worked in the City. But life is different for Russians, they look so tragic, even when drunk, and so one went on respecting old Shuvarov for earning his living. He did this amazing feat by going about doing ghastly drawings of his friends Lady This and Lady That, which he somehow sold to the illustrated journals of the week, where they appeared in all sorts of colours under headings like "The Third of Five Lovely Sisters" or "Popular Daughter of a Great American," and boldly signed "Shuvarov."

He was everywhere, in a quiet and pleasant way. Sometimes he was at Fay Avalon's, but only sometimes at Fay Avalon's. Superior people who had read Dostoeffsky called him Nicholas Pavlovitch, which is of course the proper way to address a Russian gentleman; while others just called him Shove-off, though not as though they meant it, for every one liked him. Women found him attractive. These Russians, they said, are so Sombre. Mrs. Mountjenkins said he had Magnetism. "One can feel it," she said, "when he comes into a room." Lady Carnal said he was charming and so *sound*.

In Prince Nicholas Pavlovitch Shuvarov, then, Mrs. Avalon found romance. No breath of scandal had ever been breathed against her, and no such breath was breathed now. Her purity and her lovely aloofness were landmarks of London society in the second decade of this century. Colonel Repington, you will remember, remarked them in particular. During the period of the war alone he sat beside her thirty-eight times for luncheon, twenty-eight times for dinner, not to speak of the innumerable times when he said "Good-evening" to her in such a way that she not only heard him but answered him. He reports a conversation in which Fay Avalon was distinctly heard to say to the Home Secretary that she detested all secret vices like drugs and love, especially middle-aged love.

"One should live in public," said Mrs. Avalon. "It is the private life that has ruined so many great lives and rotted so many good brains."

"Quite," said the Home Secretary. "Quite." But in a few days he had to resign owing to liver trouble—so it was said—and Mrs. Avalon fell in love with Prince N. P. Shuvarov. Her one lapse, you understand. All her life she had longed for this one thing, romance; and at last it had come, in the sombre eyes of a stranger.

Mrs. Avalon did not know much about that Kind of Thing—the "private life"—but she knew a good deal about her friends, and that was a good deal more than she intended they should know about her. She organised her life to suit her love. It sounds beastly, that, but then you do not know Fay Avalon and I do, and that is why I know that nothing she did could ever be so beastly as if any one else did it, for she was a darling. As for Prince Shuvarov, he was Russian all the way and could organise nothing. She adored that. . . .

## II

Never, never, did they go anywhere together: neither to the play, nor to a restaurant, nor to a ball; and only very seldom was he at her house, a guest among many. But every afternoon Fay Avalon would steal to her lover's studio in a quiet street in Hampstead. Not, of course, in her car, but in a taxi.

And what a relief it was, to enter the dim, bare silence of

that studio! The clatter of the voices of the luncheon-party she had just left faded instantly from her mind, a lovely mist came in between the unquiet delight of her heart and the usual labours of her life. She rested on a divan in a corner of that secret studio, while Shuvarov would pace about in his feverish way. It was a very bare studio, but it would not have remained so bare if she had had her way. Though, indeed, Fay Avalon, she who had so despised "the private life," would have been shocked, she simply could not have helped being shocked, if he had not impatiently dismissed her offer to make of the studio a pavilion worthy of Babylonian lovers. "I make just enough money not to starve," said Shuvarov. "And that is enough for any man."

They were, of course, quite often unhappy, for Russians are like that. There were scenes, introspective and bitter, there were accusations, quarrels, reconciliations. It was some time before Mrs. Avalon realised that it is in the Slav Temperament to make violent scenes about nothing and then to yield adorably to passionate reconciliations. It was rather wearing for the nerves, she protested. "You have lived smoothly for too long," he retorted in a harsh moment. "You have known no wretchedness, Fay, because you have *felt* nothing! God, you Englishwomen! In Russia our women *live*, they *feel*. . . ."

But Fay Avalon only sighed at that, certain that no woman anywhere could feel so much as she . . . and she was a little afraid for herself, the way this thing she had not known before, this thing called love, had taken hold of her.

One day their privacy suffered a shock. Mrs. Avalon had just left the studio, in the evening, and had turned the corner into a more fequented street in search for a taxi, when a tall, shabby young man confronted her. He stood before her so that she could not pass, and his face mocked her, a lean face made very sinister by his nose, perhaps a fine nose once but now broken so that it inclined noticeably to one side. He examined her with a sneer in his eyes. She did not at first know it for a sneer, for no man had ever sneered at Fay Avalon before. He swept off his hat, a sardonic gesture, and he replaced it. It was a soft, dirty, dilapidated hat of the rakish sort, such as has been worn by every pirate that has ever been heard of.

"Good-evening, Mrs Avalon," said the shabby young man.

"I am afraid . . ." doubtfully began Fay Avalon.

"Not at all!" said the shabby young man. He smiled graciously.

"It is my misfortune," he said, "that we have not been introduced. I have not been going about very much in society lately, because of one thing and another. And I called you by your name merely to show you that I know who you are. I also know where you have been. I can't, of course, say that I know exactly what you have been doing, but I can't help thinking that your husband would have no doubt about it. Husbands are like that, madam. Juries are also like that. I wonder, Mrs. Avalon, if you will think me very boorish if I, well, insist on your lending me fifty pounds?"

The young man was very shabbily dressed, but he was so very unpleasant, so entirely and symmetrically unpleasant, that, she thought, he must once have been a gentleman. She stared at him, and she shivered a little. Perhaps, she thought, this is the first man I have ever met who has simply no desire to please me. Perhaps most men are only possible because they desire to please women. This one is unaffectedly foul. . . .

"You are blackmailing me, then?" she asked him: and her voice did not tremble more than ever so little.

"Yes," said the shabby young man. "And I am doing it as unpleasantly as I know how. I am sure, Mrs. Avalon, that you had rather I was unpleasant than that I made love, like the greasy blackmailers one meets in books. And, anyhow, I could not possibly compete with Prince Nicholas Pavlovitch Shuvarov. These foreigners, I am told, have the technique. . ."

She stared at him with unbelieving eyes. Could there be men

such as this, so foul! To what awful depths of bitterness must this revolting man have sunk, that he could so wantonly and cruelly insult a stranger!

"I realise you dislike me very much," said the young man with the broken nose. "But, even so, I should prefer that that matter of the fifty pounds should engage your attention more or less immediately."

Mrs. Avalon shivered a little.

"Don't, please, speak any more!" she breathed at last. "You seem to know so much that I am sure you know the address of my house. The telephone-book will, however, provide you with any details that may have escaped your attention. If you will call at noon to-morrow you will be given an envelope at the door. May I pass now, please?"

"Why, of course!" said he, and stood aside.

But somehow she did not pass immediately. She stared into his face with very wide, childish eyes, and there was a queer sort of hurt smile crucified in their depths.

"I have never been spoken to like this before," she said. "Who are you?"

"I am the cavalier of the streets, madam," said the tall shabby man with the broken nose. She stared at him very thoughtfully.

"And is that a good thing to be?"

The cavalier of the streets smiled curiously.

"I had thought, Mrs. Avalon, that it was I who was detaining you. . . ."

"You see," said Mrs. Avalon gently, "you are the vilest man I have ever met. You are probably the vilest man in the world, and so I am curious. You will have your fifty pounds. Or would you not prefer a hundred?"

But the ice of Fay Avalon did not freeze the cavalier of the streets.

"I do not accept presents from ladies," he said. "Fifty is business, but the extra fifty is an insult to a gentleman." He smiled right into her face. "You may pass, Mrs. Avalon."

"You are a gentleman? You were, perhaps you mean?"

"A gentleman," said the shabby young man, "is a man who is never *unintentionally* rude to any one. I am a gentleman."

He stood aside, and swept off his dilapidated hat. She took one step, two, three. . . .

"I do hope," she murmured swiftly, "that I will never see you again."

The lean, weathered face with the fantastic nose mocked her. Fay Avalon had never been mocked before.

"Didn't I tell you," he said, "that I was the cavalier of the streets? I am alone, the solitary supporter of chivalry and all manner of outdoor manliness. Thus, it will be very difficult to resist the pleasure of seeing you again, Mrs. Avalon, for you are, without a doubt, a darling. But I will try to resist it, really I will. . . ."

"Please," said Mrs. Avalon, and went swiftly.

### III

The next afternoon Mrs. Avalon had promised to appear at a charity *matinée* in a playful duologue between Cleopatra and a hearty gentleman alleged to be Mark Antony's valet; and as she had never gone to the trouble of acquiring a reputation as Unreliable—in fact, Fay Avalon was born with "careless habits of accuracy"—and though she was feeling less like Cleopatra than she had ever felt in her life, it was only after she had done her duty by the charity *matinée* that she set out for the quiet street in Hampstead.

She gave Nicholas Pavlovitch only the bald outline of the beastly happening. Blackmailer, money. He blushed furiously. Often she had seen him blush, but never as now. He was like a child who has just been smacked and knows he has not deserved it. He couldn't, he said, bear the indecency, the shame, of it . . . that, through loving him, she should have to endure this awful thing. There was only one thing to do. She must "cut him out," that's all! And how funnily tragic that slang sounded in his twisted Russian pronunciation.

She laughed at that. Not much, but just enough. "We do not," she said, "take our tragedies so tragically. But scratch a Russian and you find a baby . . ." She kissed him.

"It is easier than that," she explained. "You must move, dear. For weeks you have been complaining of the lighting in this studio—and now you have every excuse for taking steps about leaving it. Long steps are preferable, Nicholas. From Hampstead to Chelsea, in fact. . . ."

Shove-off took steps at once, and these lead him to a little studio in a little street off the King's Road, Chelsea. It was a little street like another, with a pillar-box at one end and the noise of buses at the other. Near the pillar-box was a lamp-post. And one autumn evening, as Mrs. Avalon walked from her lover's studio into Cheyne Walk, she saw a man leaning against the lamp-post, and under a soft dilapidated hat she saw the shape of a lean face and a broken nose. He was motionless, indifferent, and he was not looking at her but at the wind that blew the leaves about the little street. Her heart jumped, and then was as still as a cut flower.

"So!" she whispered bitterly. "Blackmailers are like history, then!"

The vile person made the courteous gesture.

"Mr. Beerbohm has it," the vile person said gravely, "that it is not history that repeats itself but historians who repeat one another. A charming writer, don't you think?"

"Oh, dear!" said Mrs. Avalon very miserably, "I thought you were vile! But I am disappointed in you. I actually thought you would leave me alone. You are even viler than I thought, you who call yourself the cavalier of the streets!"

"Perhaps," murmured the shabby young man. "Perhaps. It seems always to have been my fate to find out the indecencies of decent people, and so, of course, decent people do not take a very liberal view of me. You find me this evening, Mrs. Avalon, in a conversational vein."

There was a ghastly sort of subtlety in his neglect to mention why he was there, a thin, rakish hawk by the lamp-post. Impotent, she loathed him. And she passed him resolutely, with a very proud face, one step, two, three. . . . And then his voice fell harshly on her back:

"You are the kind of woman men dream about in lonely moments. My life is made of lonely moments, and I think this is the loneliest of all. Go away quickly, Fay Avalon!"

Bewilderment wheeled her round.

"*What* did you say?" she cried.

But he stood as when she had first seen him, the silhouette of a hawk with a broken nose, and he stared not at her but at the wind that blew the leaves about the little street.

"It is not worth repeating," he said sharply into the middle air. "But to what I said, I added 'Go very quickly,' and I meant it— for your sake. This is a lonely place, Mrs. Avalon, and the cavalier of the streets is as nearly an outlaw as any one outside a cinema. It is a long time since I kissed a lady, and the only thing that restrains me from doing it now is the fact that I have never in my life kissed any one who did not wish to be kissed by me. So you had better go quickly, Fay Avalon."

She went, as swiftly as a shadow.

## IV

Mrs. Avalon, after her first horrid experience, had had the forethought to keep in her jewel-safe a roll of Bank of England notes. That evening, having sent her maid from the room, she counted out five notes from the roll. She smiled wryly . . . "And so," she thought, "this is hell. And Fay Avalon is well in it, she is in a very ghastly hell." Very slowly, very absently, she recounted the five ten-pound notes. They were clean and crisp and delicious, marvellously above the funny stuff that passes for money in France and America. They were symbols of a spacious England, of splendid adventurers and gallant merchantmen, they were symbols of all the luxuries of *race* and manners, dead now except in the hearts of a few shy people. A Bank of England note is the cleanest expression money has ever acquired, it is more than money, it decorates money. Only one of the five notes that passed through Mrs. Avalon's fingers bore even a sign that other human hands had ever touched them, and that was but a little splash as of red ink on its back.

She put them in an envelope, wrote "To C.O.S." across it, and privily instructed the butler that he give it into the hands of the person who had already called once before and who *might* call again towards noon the following morning.

"The gentleman called, madam," said Smith the next morning, when she came in from a walk for luncheon.

"The gentleman, Smith?"

"He had that manner, madam."

"There will be ten for luncheon, not eight, Smith."

"Major Cypress and Mr. Trevor rang up to inquire if you expected them to luncheon, madam. They seemed, I think, disappointed that you did not."

"They rang up together?"

"Such was my impression, madam. They said that there must be some mistake about your not expecting them to luncheon as they had not been asked to luncheon anywhere else. On asking my opinion as to whether, if they called at about half-past one, you would or would not ask them to stay, I ventured to say, madam, that it was very probable. I gather that that will make twelve for luncheon, madam."

Mrs. Avalon smiled. "Very good, Smith."

"The gentleman who called left this letter, madam."

"Put it down over there. That will do, Smith, thank you."

When she was alone she gingerly touched the letter. It was not addressed. The expression on her face was as though she was breathing the air of a pest-house.

"I see," said the note, "that you think me even viler than I am. That is what I intended. By giving me money when I did not ask for it, you have made the profession of blackmailer an impossible one for a man of sensibility. Good-bye."

V

She did not tell Nicholas Pavlovitch of this second encounter. It would, she thought, be only disturbing him for nothing, for she was quite convinced that she had now seen the last of the cavalier of the streets. She couldn't help having a little private conceit about it. After all, not every woman would have managed that foul man so—certainly not those notoriously managing women who know How to deal with men. "Oh, dear!" she thought, "I am clever, I really am!" Even this man, so brutally undesirous to please, had been charmed back into the loathsome shades whence he had so horridly come—so impressed had he been by her original way of being blackmailed that he had been appalled into respectful invisibility. She had, after all, allowed herself to be blackmailed charmingly, she had been as charming as any woman being blackmailed could possibly be.

It was because of such thoughts that, eleven evenings later, she was so particularly angry: for the lamp-light near the pillar-box fell on the figure of the cavalier of the streets, the careless, rakish figure at his disgusting post. By the beating of her heart, she knew him yards and yards away. Still she stood for one long moment, to quiet her heart, and then, intolerantly, she swept on. She was humiliated in a most private conceit. She was angrier than she had ever been in her life.

Swiftly she pressed on, to pass him with inexpressible contempt; but the pavement was narrow, and wide the sweep of the bad man's hat.

"Forgive me," said he. "I had not intended to worry you again, but—"

"You do not *worry* me," said a lady to an insect.

"In that case," said the cavalier of the streets, "I may spare you my apologies, which, I assure you, are quite dangerously insincere. I had intended not to sin against you again. But, this very afternoon, something has happened, something really rather awkward. I do not often lose money at poker, Mrs. Avalon—in fact I make a point of not losing money at poker, in so far, of course, as a man of honour may make a point about a hazard. But, whether it was the memory of your beauty, for I may not ever forget it, that came between me and my skill, or whether— Oh, what does it matter why it was, since the fact remains that I have lost money, and must pay what I owe or forfeit my honour. . . ."

"Your *honour!*" she gasped. "Oh, *commedia, commedia!*"

"I could wish I was as privileged as you to take a comical view of it. It is only a small debt, however. A matter of twenty pounds. I have still ten left of the fifty you so kindly lent to me the other day—I wonder, Mrs. Avalon, I wonder if you could by any chance help me with the rest? I should be so grateful."

So she had been right about him, after all! He would not have come again, in the ordinary way. She looked into his eyes, and they were as the eyes of other men. The cavalier of the streets was without his sneer.

"Yes," she said gravely. "A debt of honour—surely you must pay a debt of honour, O cavalier of the streets! It is very commendable in you to want to."

"It is merely good sense, madam. Like all matters of honour. If one does not pay, one does not get paid."

Her fingers were playing within her bag. They ceased.

"I'm so afraid," she murmured, "that I have only a few shillings. . ."

"Pity!" whispered the shabby young man; and he smiled

curiously, as might a man whose horse has been beaten by a short head.

"I will go home," said Fay Avalon, "and get you the money."

"You will do nothing of the sort, Mrs. Avalon. Ridiculous to put you to that trouble for a mere ten pounds. Besides, it might cause comment if I showed myself at your door again."

"My butler thought you charming," she told him gravely.

"Therein he discerned your influence over me, Mrs. Avalon. No, I have a better idea! Go back to Prince Shuvarov and ask him to—"

"But he is so poor!"

"Heavens, those insufferable drawings of his must sometimes fetch some money! Try, please. It is only fair, after all, that he should contribute a little towards my support—"

"Your debt of honour, surely!"

"I am rebuked. A man's honour would be very adequately preserved by you, Mrs. Avalon. But please do as I suggest. I will abide by the weight of Shuvarov's pocket."

With a quick gesture, she left him. She found Shuvarov preparing to shave, for when he was dining out he always shaved twice, like all proper men. She did not give him time to voice his surprise at her re-entrance.

"That wretch is here again," she explained swiftly. "I know you are poor, dear, but have you just a few pounds you could lend me? Ten, for instance?"

Shuvarov began furiously, his cheeks mantling. "That man . . ." He waved his shaving-brush.

"Never mind that now, dear. Have you or haven't you the money? Please, Nicholas?" She was always gentle with him. He was such a child.

Nicholas Pavlovitch shrugged his shoulders, and banged down the shaving-brush.

"You are encouraging him," he said fatalistically. "Lucky I sold a drawing for just that amount to-day. Lucky for that man, I mean." He fumbled in his waistcoat pocket, and gave her a banknote.

"Bless you, Nicholas!" she cried softly, and was going, when the light fell on the banknote in her hand so that there was visible on it a little splash as of red ink. . . .

Slowly, she looked up at Prince Nicholas Pavlovitch Shuvarov. Her lips did not move, but he understood, and his thin, handsome face went as white as a soiled handkerchief.

The cavalier of the streets saw her face as she approached. She flung the note at him, so that it fell from his jacket to his feet. She passed him. But fingers swiftly clutched her arm, so that it hurt.

"That," he said harshly, "will teach a lovely lady to love scum. I intended that it should. He and I arranged the *coup*, ages ago. But when I saw you the first time, in Hampstead, I sickened. That is why I was so beastly, that you should hate me as much as I hated myself. *Le coup est nul*, I told Shuvarov after that. Since then your face has haunted me. So I did this—to cure you of your silly infatuation for a man who would eat into your life like a foul little worm into a lovely fruit. God, how you could ever have liked that lousy, half-baked, professional Russian! I saw him to-day, and saw that he still had the note with the red mark on it—this!" And he ground his heel on the note on the pavement. Tighter he held her arm, and he scowled into her face. She thought of the wet-white she would have to use on her arm to hide the bruises of his fingers.

"You're hurting me!" she cried.

"I know. I have sinned against you," he said, "but you have done worse. You have sinned against yourself. Now go, and sin no more. And you'd better go damn quick else you'll be very late for dinner and the old K.C. will get cross."

"*You* to talk of sin!" she cried, and laughed.

"Naturally, Fay Avalon. For only Satan can rebuke sin with authority."

"Oh, pouf!" she laughed. "You are sentimental then!"

"Hell!" snapped the cavalier of the streets. "I am in love!" And as he swept off his dilapidated hat she could not help a thought that a plume would wave more becomingly from that particular hat than from any other hat she knew or would ever know. Romance. . . .

"Oh, dear!" sighed Mrs. Avalon. "Good-bye." But the cavalier was already only a distant shadow in the street.

# Major Cypress goes off the Deep End

## I

This story has no point. No story that has anything to do with Hugo Cypress could have a point, for Hugo is an utterly pointless man. Dear Hugo. . . .

I have known him since he was so high, and as I was also so high, I know him well. I could tell you of many little happenings, just to show you the sort of man he was, but one in particular, a martial one, vividly occurs to me. It was in the third year of the war, and I had been shoved into the War Office, because of a personal application of that great scientific truth to the effect that two things cannot be in the same place at once, particularly if one of them happens to be a German shell; and, one day, Hugo called. His arm was in a sling and a light was in his eye. Dear Hugo. . . .

"Show me," said Hugo, "a man who will give me a job of work."

I showed him old Tornado Toby—officially known as Major-General Sir Tobias Blast, K.C.M.G., D.S.O., M.V.O., O.U.D.S., etc. I stood in a far corner, and was very silent.

"What d'you want?" said Sir Toby.

"Job of work, sir."

"Where?"

"Commission going to Iraq, sir."

"Why?"

"Don't know, sir. But it's going."

"Idiot. Why d'you want the job?"

"Chap must have a job of work, sir."

Tornado Toby looked him over contemptuously, and his eye roved from the crown on Hugo's shoulder-strap to the bits of ribbon on Hugo's sleeve and the light in Hugo's eye.

"What's the matter with you as you are?"

"Fired out, sir. Sick."

Sir Toby's eye at last came to rest on Hugo's disabled arm. He drew a blank form towards him. I played about with a cigarette-case.

"You can smoke," he snarled. "What are they?"

"Virginian, sir."

"Pah! You can't smoke."

He looked at Hugo.

"Sit down, Major."

"Thank you, sir."

Sir Toby poised pencil over paper.

"Education?"

"None, sir."

"Where were you educated?"

"Nowhere, sir."

"Idiot. Where were you at school?"

"Eton, sir."

"Shake," said Sir Toby.

They shook.

"What qualifications for this job in Iraq? Think before you answer."

"Thank you, sir."

Hugo thought.

"Can't think of any, sir," he said at last.

"Languages? French?"

"Very guarded, sir."

"Can you live on your pay?"

"Live on anything, sir."

"Hum! Any private means?"

"Very private, sir. Never seen them."

"How d'you live in London, then?"

"Pretty well, sir."

Hugo got that job, and in 1919 he came back to England, very bronzed and lean and gay. But the gaiety did not last very long.

Now Hugo, in the days of his first youth, had been consumed by an ambition to be regarded as the kind of man to whom no chaste woman should be allowed to speak. But nothing ever came of that, he never even succeeded in persuading a chaste woman to cut him; wherefore in the course of time he came to think of himself as a poor harmless idiot who was liked by every one and loved by none. "Dear Hugo," people said. That was all right in its way, said Hugo, but he was not so young as he had been and it got, he said, on his nerves a bit. . . .

Soon after he had returned from the Near East, and when the gaiety had worn off, he discovered a pressing desire to Settle Down. And he cast a keen eye round and about the fair land of Britain, and behold! he saw Miss Shirley St. George—and, still worse, got it into his head that she had seen him. Immediately, he fell in love with Miss Shirley St. George. He had, of course, no money: she had no money. He proposed to her: she refused him. He begged: she laughed. "Dear Hugo," she said.

## II

Now Miss Shirley St. George was little sister to George Tarlyon, whom I think I've told you about.

One morning Hugo arose from his bed in the chambers, which he could not afford, and directed the valet, whom he could not afford, to send this telephone message: "Major Cypress desires to see Lord Tarlyon at his club at once."

"Lord Tarlyon," came the answer, "will see Major Cypress at Lord Tarlyon's club at Lord Tarlyon's convenience, and desires Major Cypress to stand at attention when speaking to him."

There are many clubs in Saint James's Street, but there is one in particular, towards the northern part, much referred to by biographers of persons of *ton* of more elegant times. Thither, that morning at a reasonable hour, went Major Cypress, very thoughtfully. Tarlyon was there. Tarlyon was always there, at a reasonable hour.

"Bronx or Martini, Hugo?"

"Sherry, thanks."

"Nice morning, Hugo. Up late last night?"

"No," said Major Cypress. "No. I was not up late last night, George. And if you really want to know, I think it is a very classy morning."

"Well," said Tarlyon, "you can't say fairer than that, old man."

Silence. . . .

"Sir," said Major Cypress, "have I your permission to pay my addresses to your little sister with a view to a matrimonial entanglement?"

"Ho!" said Tarlyon.

"What the devil do you mean by saying 'Ho!' when I ask you if I can pay my—"

"You can pay her what you like," said Tarlyon sulkily.

"I thank you," said Hugo.

"But," said Tarlyon, "can you pay her anything at all? Major Cypress, are you in a position to support a wife?"

"Well, I never!" gasped Hugo. "I'm on half-pay, man!"

"Ho!" said Tarlyon. "I withdraw my consent. I hate to be unkind to majors, but I'm afraid I must. How are you going to live, man?"

"Can't worry about cheques in Paradise, George."

"Good for you, old Hugo! Very pretty. Bronx or Martini?"

"Sherry, thanks. George, you don't know what love is. . . ."

"Keep nothing from me, Hugo. What is love? Ah, what is love? I insist on being told. . . ."

"Love," said Hugo, "is proposing to Shirley five times in five months and being rejected five times in five months . . . O God!"

"What did the girl say?"

"Say! She laughed at me, George. Five times running! 'Dear Hugo . . .' That's what she said!"

"Poor old Hugo!"

"She said, George, that she could never, never marry me. . . ."

"Well, damn it, man, you didn't take that lying down, did you! And you a Major!"

"I took it lightly, George. I smiled. I distinctly remember smiling. O God!"

"I *am* so sorry, Hugo! I really am, you know. Honestly, old man, I'd sooner have you for a brother-in-law than any man alive— except, perhaps, a Rockefeller."

"Money, George, isn't everything."

"You're right there, old man. Your money is completely nothing, anyhow. What's your next step? Orchids?"

"I am no good at those Dago tricks, George."

"Shirley's very partial to carnations, old man."

"No, George. Not even carnations. She'd laugh at me. She'd say 'dear Hugo' . . ."

"Well, old man, you might go further and hear worse. It's purple carnations she's especially fond of, by the way."

"George, I'm going to try just once again—without carnations. Just once more, old man. And I thought I'd get your backing."

"Full and square, Hugo, it's with you. The cheek of that girl! Shall I ring her up and. . . ."

"For God's sake don't! But you're a good fellow, George . . . I say, if she refuses me again I don't know what I'll do."

"Have a drink, old man. Bronx, sherry, or Martini?"

"No more, thanks."

"Well, best of luck, old man!"

"Thank you, George. Good-bye."

"See you this evening?"

"Look here, old man, I don't want to be dramatic and all that, but you may never see me again." And Hugo was stone-cold serious. He was probably the most serious man in England at that moment.

"Good-bye, old man. Thanks so much."

"Just a moment." And George Tarlyon went to the writing-table, rapidly wrote a short note, and put the envelope into Hugo's hand.

"Give that to Shirley," said he. But Hugo looked suspicious.

"It's about the theatre to-night," explained Tarlyon. "I'm taking her to *Loyalties*, to improve her mind."

"Ah," said Hugo. "*Loyalties*! Ah! Jew play. Very improving." Hugo thought weightily.

"Look here," said Hugo, "you know about these things—you were born to be a co-respondent, George. Got any tips to give a chap?"

"There's only one, old Hugo—take 'em young and treat 'em rough. Hairy, primitive man business, you know. 'Come here, woman, and I'll learn you' stuff. But it works better with some than with others, and it's rather risky. You might try giving her a thick ear, though—only in fun, of course. Cat playing with mouse *motif*. Tender brutality's your line, Hugo. Many a good woman's been won by a little tender brutality tastefully applied. Just put it to her gently that you'll give her a thick ear unless she accepts you. You can always lead the conversation to ears, somehow. . . . Well, good-bye. Luck, Hugo. Hey, don't forget your hat!"

### III

Miss Shirley St. George lived with her aunt in Audley Square, Tarlyon saying that he was no fit person for a young girl to live with, and the aunt agreeing. They adored each other, George and Shirley.

Towards Audley Square walked Major Cypress, very thought-fully. Piccadilly had to be crossed, from the new Wolseley building to Mr. Solomon's, the florist. Piccadilly was crossed, miraculously, for the traffic was thick, though genial. A newsboy yelled "Execution of Erskine Childers" into his ear.

"Boy," said Major Cypress, "you must not do that. You must not gloat on death like that, and before perfect strangers, too. And, besides, though you may not have shared Mr. Childers's political opinions, you must admit that he did not die meanly. Here's a shilling for you, and don't let me hear you talking so much about executions in future."

Major Cypress then walked away a pace or two, and stood before the flower-laden windows of Mr. Solomon. The boy watched him.

"Balmy," said the boy.

"Mysterious disappearance of Child!" yelled the boy.

"Damn it," thought Major Cypress. "I am in love. Oh, damn it!"

And he stared into the flower-laden windows of Mr. Solomon. Orchids there were therein, yellow and mauve and speckled. Roses, little, tight autumn roses. Pink and white anemones, hyacinths and jonquils, white Dutch lilacs and fat chrysanthemums in white and bronze. And there were carnations—right in the middle of that pageant was a splash of purple carnations.

"Carnations," thought Major Cypress. "And, in particular, purple carnations. But that is not a proper way for an Englishman to win a wife. A little tender brutality is the way. But how to be tenderly brutal? Hell, I wish I was a Frenchman! A gardenia, on the other hand, may not come amiss. I will wear a gardenia. It will give me an air of high-minded depravity, which, they say, is attractive to young women."

Major Cypress entered within, and in due course was served with a gardenia.

"For your button-hole, sir?"

"I suppose so," said Major Cypress. "But not so much vegetable matter with it, please. I want a gardenia, not a garden. Thank you."

"Thank you, sir. Nice morning, sir."

"I doubt it," said Major Cypress.

He wandered westwards, past the Berkeley. The commissionaire at the restaurant doors saluted him. Hugo liked that, and always rather sought it. Tarlyon was of opinion that the commissionaire probably mistook him for some one who had once tipped him, but Hugo said that that was not the point, while to be saluted by commissionaires on Piccadilly was a thing that happened only to very few people.

## IV

At last, very thoughtfully, he came to the house in Audley Square. As he rang, a clock struck one and gave him an idea.

"I will ask her to luncheon at Claridge's," he thought. "It will be a good opening."

Major Cypress waited in the drawing-room for quite a long time. He paced about. The floor was of parquet, mostly uncovered, and so his feet made a noise. He sat down.

"You again!" cried Shirley.

"How are you, Shirley?"

"I refuse to tell you, Hugo. I am tired of telling you. Don't I look well?"

"Hum," said Hugo. He could never answer questions like that.

Shirley came near. She was in a sort of bronze dress of *crêpe marocain*, and her throat glowed very white. Her face Major Cypress did not actually look at, it tempted him so exceedingly. Shirley smiled.

"I will tell you," she smiled, "what you have come to do, Hugo. You have come to take me out to lunch."

"I do wish," said Hugo, "that you would get out of that nasty habit of calling 'luncheon' lunch. Lunch sounds like a glass of milk and a digestive biscuit."

"Dear Hugo!"

"Look here, Shirley, don't ever say that again!"

Shirley was very near, and her white hands were somehow like white flowers. But at her face he did not look.

"Dea—"

"Don't!" he roared.

Now Shirley was twenty and tall and straight and fair, and when she laughed you saw why servants were polite to her on sight. And oh, she was such a pretty girl!

"Hugo," she said, "you are going to propose to me again."

"Oh, am I!"

"Yes," she said, "you are. And if you say you are not, then you are a liar, and I don't like liars."

Then something happened to Hugo Cypress; and, after all, he was thirty-four, and she only twenty. He glared down at Shirley St. George, and from his mouth issued reasonable and critical noises, as befitted a man of thirty-four who has offered his hand five times running to a slip of a girl of twenty.

"Shirley," he said, "listen to me. You are a very pretty young lady. I have so far been so shy with you that I have not been able to tell you how beautiful I think you are—"

"Thank you, Hugo," she said very softly. And she tempted him exceedingly, but he continued on his manly way, glaring at a point half-way between her right ear and her left shoulder.

"Nor have I been able to tell you, Shirley, how I love you. That was because I was shy—but I have now finished with being shy. I adore you so frightfully, my dear, that I have made myself a carpet for you to walk on. And you have taken advantage of me, that's what you've done. Carpets get frayed. You have treated me, Shirley, exactly as a heartless, meretricious woman of thirty might treat an infatuated soap-manufacturer. That is, perhaps, because you are used to men being in love with you, and know that they will love you all the more the worse you treat them. Perhaps you are right, Shirley. But I can't bear it any more, and so I am now going to leave this building and your life. . . ." And Hugo went towards the door with a firm step.

"You're not going, Hugo!" It was a cry.

"I am indeed, Shirley. Good-bye. And God bless you."

"Oh, dear, every man says 'God bless you!'" cried Shirley. "It is the most final and most bitter thing they can say, for they say it with a prayer to the devil in their hearts. Go away, Hugo Cypress. I hate you."

"That's why I am saying good-bye, Shirley."

"But surely you can't go without proposing to me for the sixth and last time!" And that was a cry.

Hugo opened the door; and he smiled, in a sort of way.

"I thought I couldn't, Shirley—but I find I can."

"But you can't, you simply can't!" she cried. "Why, I came down to see you on the distinct understanding that you were going to propose to me for the sixth and last time and only *then* going away for ever! Hugo, you can't do one without the other—it's not fair!"

"Don't worry, little Shirley. The day is yet young, and some one else is sure to propose to you in the course of it. You will observe, my dear, that I am being cynical, after the manner of all rejected young men."

"But, Hugo, I want *you* to—for the sixth and last time, dear, just to see what I'll say!" And she tempted him exceedingly with her sun-lit face.

"That's just it, Shirley. I know what you'll say. Good-bye."

"Oh, oh!" cried Shirley. "How awful men are! And how d'you know what I'll say, Hugo? You are a clever chap, aren't you? Are you a psycho-analyst, Hugo? Can you tell what is passing in a woman's mind by looking at her instep? And for heaven's sake don't go on standing in that doorway looking like a draught!"

"Sorry, Shirley." And Hugo faded away round the angle of the door and was closing it behind him.

"Hugo, how dare you go like that!" And that was the most frantic cry of all; and Hugo's face reappeared round the angle of the door, and it was a rather bewildered face.

"Well, damn it, my dear, I must go somehow!"

"Yes, but you know very well you can't live without me—don't you, Hugo? Now answer truthfully, Hugo."

"Well, you know, since you came in this morning, I've been thinking it over—"

"But how awful you are to admit that you can think of anything when you're with Shirley!"

"There you go!" he cried harshly. "Making a fool of me!"

"But, my darling, I must make someth—"

"What was that you said?" he snapped.

"Have you gone mad? Didn't you hear me?"

"Child, did you or did you not call me 'darling'?"

"Why, so I did! I'm so sorry, Hugo. . . ."

Hugo Cypress advanced across the room and towered above Shirley St. George.

"Are you playing the fool, Shirley?"

"I am playing for time, my darling—lunch-time. Luncheon-time, I mean."

She giggled.

Now Shirley was not given to giggling. . . .

No one had ever seen Shirley carrying an umbrella, and no one had ever heard Shirley giggling.

"Ho!" muttered Major Cypress.

"Don't gargle in my aunt's drawing-room, Hugo!"

"I'm thinking, Shirley."

"Don't think!" she cried sharply.

"Well," he began, and stopped.

"Wipe your forehead, dear; you're rather hot." Hugo wiped his forehead.

"Look here, Shirley, supposing—just supposing—that I so far forget myself as to prop—"

"Oh, Hugo!" And she clapped her hand—little Shirley! "You must! For the sixth and last time . . . just to make it even numbers!"

Hugo's face was as white as his gardenia.

"For the sixth and last time, Shirley, will you marry me?"

As she stood, with the palms of her hands pressed down on the table and her little face thrown back, she was like a dove, still and absorbed. She was absorbed in something that was Hugo, yet in something that was much more than Hugo. And then her lips trembled a little; they whispered:

"Oh, Hugo, I have been such a beast! But you are so sweet that I simply couldn't help it!"

He didn't understand.

But he understood when suddenly she crooked an arm around his neck and brought his face down to hers, and he saw that her eyes were wet. . . .

"My God!" he said, and kissed her bravely.

"Of course," she whispered. "Of course. . . ."

"No, not like that," she whispered. "Not as though I were your sister. I beg you to observe that I am not your sister. Yes, properly, dear. Oh, I do like you frightfully, Hugo. . . ."

Then quite a lot of things happened at the same time; and then he cried:

"But why didn't you tell me before?"

"Because I didn't realise, my darling. I didn't know I loved you—and how can a girl know a thing like that? Oh, Hugo, you are so sweet! What fun to have you for keeps! And it will be nice to chew bits of you now and then—Oh, what fun we'll have! Dear Hugo. . . ."

"And you said, Shirley, that you would never, never marry me!"

"I didn't know myself, dear—nor you! Until, after the fifth time, when you went away saying that you would never come back. And then I was very sorry, Hugo."

"Oh, by the way," he said, "here's a note from George—about taking you to *Loyalties* to-night."

She read the note.

"Oh!" she said.

"What does he say?" he asked.

She tore up the note.

"Only that he's got a box for *Loyalties*, and that I may ask whom I like—"

"Thanks so much, Shirley. I'd love to come. It will improve my mind."

Now this was the note from George Tarlyon to his little sister, Shirley St. George:

"Shirley, how dare you go about London refusing to marry such of my friends, if any, who ask you? 'Never, never,' indeed! Remember, Shirley, that there's only one bigger lie than 'never, never,' and that is 'always, always.'"

"Oh!" thought Shirley. "Fat lot he knows about it!" But all the same, she never said 'always, always'; she just thought it.

The rest of this story is quite uninteresting, for Hugo and Shirley were happy ever after: which is, unfortunately, more than most people are, what with first one thing and then another. . . .

# Consuelo Brown

It is told by young Raymond Paris, the novelist:

A few days after my arrival at the hotel on the hill behind Algiers, where I intended to stay some time for reasons best known to myself, I wrote to a friend in London, Ralph Trevor, telling him of the place and the people, and, in particular, of the people in my hotel. I must explain that I am a traveller of ignoble inclinations, so that my descent on Africa was in every way very dissimilar from that of Mrs. Rosita Forbes. I cannot lay claim to a very adventurous spirit—though, of course, I am always ready to make a fourth, a third, or a second, as the case may be but only too seldom is. What I mean to say is that on my arrival in Algiers, instead of hiring a room so situated in the town that I could see or smell its Arab activities, I straightway made for the large building which dominates the hill of Mustapha: and which has about as much relation to Algeria as the Carlton at Cannes, the Paris at Monte Carlo, or the Normandy at Deauville.

There I stayed, and I wrote to my friend, describing the hotel, and the people in the hotel, and how Robert Hichens was worshipped by the directors thereof, and how they fell down before effigies of the authoress of *The Sheik*, as well they might, for who knows how many people would not go to Algeria but for *The Garden of Allah* and *The Sheik?* In particular I described an amiable gentleman, and how he looked exactly like Lord Beaverbrook might have looked if he hadn't made so much money all by himself, a sort of rugged grandeur being spread over features not otherwise remarkable; and then I went on to say that of course there was the usual hotel Pretty Girl, and very pretty she was too. "I do not know her yet," I wrote, "and I probably never will, for they tell me—the barman tells me—that she and her mother are inclined to be rather exclusive and do not mix with the other guests. Be that as it may, the girl is extraordinarily pretty in a slim, fascinating way which is quite indescribable. She must be very young, for I notice that it's only with difficulty that she manages to repress a giggle at things her mother says, which is really very nice of her, don't you think? On the other hand she dresses so amazingly well, really well, I mean, no home-made stuff, that she simply can't be under twenty— unless, of course, her mother chooses her clothes for her, but I am rather inclined to doubt that, her mother's clothes being excessively county and therefore not remarkable for *chic.* . . ." and so on and so on in a friendly way about this and that.

When next I wrote to Ralph Trevor, which was not before I had to, he having written to me several times about one thing and another, I mentioned that I had, so to speak, put the lid on the exclusive business as regards the hotel Pretty Girl and her agreeable parent. "Her name is Consuelo Brown," I wrote, "and they live not far from Leicester. If you ask me how in the world a girl who lives not far from Leicester comes to be called Consuelo, I will tell you that that is because her mother has always admired that beautiful lady who was Miss Consuelo Vanderbilt; but I am only surmising that for your benefit, for Mrs. Brown has not as yet told me the true facts of the matter. Miss Brown is English and American in equal parts, her late father having been an American Admiral. If he was anything like his daughter he must have been a very pretty Admiral.

"By the way, I was quite wrong about Miss Brown's age, she turns out to be only eighteen! And when she talks I can quite believe it, not that she is at all silly or giggly—she still deliciously represses the giggly part—but because she prefaces a good many of her remarks with an 'Oh!' which sounds exactly as though she had just eaten a piece of Turkish Delight and had liked it rather a lot. I met her at a dance given at the hotel the other night. A *Gala Bal*, they called it. A *Soirée de Gala*. Well, I wandered into the *Gala Bal*, and saw her sitting in a far corner with her mother, looking very absent-minded, I thought; and well she might, for the difference between a *Gala Bal* and a common-or-garden *Bal* is that five hundred people are shoved on to a floor made to hold fifty; and so I sidled across the floor, made my bow and formed words indicative of a pressing desire to dance with her, all of which went quite well. It went even better, when, just as we were about to take the floor, I asked her 'whether she preferred to be held by the spine or the liver?' at which she suddenly gave such a laugh that various French-women looked for the first time away from her clothes to her face, which was a very agreeable contrast to theirs, they having used powder and what-nots to excess in honour of the *Gala Bal*.

"I suppose you know what a French hotel orchestra is like at playing dance music? It is very good as an orchestra over meals, very classical and all that, but what is the use of a fox-trot without saxophones and drums and little tiddley-bits here and there? One has to be a little mad to dance a fox-trot, a little mad or a little drunk, but one can't be a little mad to the polite strains of an orchestra lead by a *chef d'orchestre*, which every now and then dries up completely to give the first violin a chance to be a first violin.

"So we gave up dancing after a while—we had to, anyhow, for the *Gala Balists* began dancing in open formation—and I lured her out on to the terrace with a promise of a lemon-squash: which, however, turned out to be an orangeade—two straws and a lump of ice, you know—but she seemed to enjoy it none the less for that. Did she like orangeade? Oh, yes, she liked orangeade frightfully. Then what to say? I asked her if she liked dancing.

"'Oh, yes!' she said very softly. 'Why, what else is there!'

"Well, when one comes to think of it, there doesn't really seem to be very much else, and so that was that. Later on, however, there turned out to be ski-ing. Oh, yes, she liked ski-ing. Dancing and ski-ing. . . . And, somehow or other, she asked me what I was, and I said 'Nothing,' which is a good deal truer than I like to think. But she said in her soft, brown way: 'Oh, how splendid! for I'm nothing, too, so we can be nothing together.' That sounded charming at the time, though now I have written it down there looks something the matter with it. But that girl is quite beyond me. . . .

"When I was eighteen I seemed to know quite a lot about girls of eighteen, but now I feel like a cow when Consuelo looks at me with her brown eyes, and my conversation with her degenerates into asking her a series of questions, like that dancing-ski-ing business. It is simply extraordinary, you know, how little one seems to know about what goes on inside girls of eighteen, and I think something ought to be done about it. I mean, one simply can't go on living one's whole life knowing nothing at all about girls of eighteen but pretending to know a whole lot about women of thirty who, on the other hand, know a good deal less than they think they do about chaps. This girl, though, is not at all a typical specimen, she can't be, for (a) she is so amazingly well-dressed, (b) she has travelled a good deal, and (c) she ran away two years ago from Heathfield, by the simple expedient of climbing the school wall at six o'clock in the evening, hailing a passing motor-lorry on the Ascot Road, and so to London and to the home not far from Leicester. And here she is now, like a flower out of season among all these elderly people, who keep on saying that they don't play bridge for money but that a shilling-a-hundred *does* lend a zest to the game. I can't help wanting, you know, to find out what she thinks of things *now*. It won't be in the least interesting to find out what she thinks of things when she is in her twenties, for her fascinating kind of beauty—you want to pass your hand

over it, that kind—can't help spoiling her, the mere daily
business of refusing proposals of marriage can't help spoiling
her—but *now*! Well, those brown eyes are the devil's own
barrier, and she's so infernally simple that one has to talk
intelligibly about everything, which is a habit one has almost
gotten out of ever since one grew up and lived among grown-
up people. Do girls of eighteen, does Consuelo, *know* anything?
I mean, does she know anything of the beauties and the dirts
that men and women do to each other in the ordinary course
of things, men and women being what they are and life being
what it is? Or does Consuelo—she allowed me to call her that,
by the way, by pulling a face when I Miss Browned her—does
Consuelo, with her slim, brown, enchanting, touchable
loveliness, know nothing about anything like that, does she
think that young men admire only with their eyes and that
therefore life is great fun? Or does she want them to admire her
with something besides their eyes and their hearts and all the
nice clean things? What does a girl of eighteen think about
when she's alone? Was Charles Garvice right or was Charles
Garvice wrong?—I am serious—about the inner thoughts of a
much admired girl of eighteen? Or are they more or less like
boys? Do girls of eighteen—really nice ones, I mean, not the
meretricious golden things one sees about London ballrooms
in July with a tremendous air of having been bored at their first
Garden Party—do the really nice ones just go fluttering on and
on until a nasty big net comes plump down on them, calling
itself Marriage and Womanhood and so on? It is all very
puzzling, I do think, and I see no reason at all for my going on
calling myself a novelist if I don't know a damn thing about
what goes on behind the brown eyes of a girl of eighteen! What
do other writers do when they are writing about girls of
eighteen? I suppose they just go on making up lies like
anything, and bitterly hope for the best. If it comes to that I am
a thundering good liar when I am put to it, but I simply

couldn't make up enough to put inside a girl like Consuelo with any hope of getting away with it. No, but it's very depressing, and me calling myself a writer. It's all right of course, when one is dealing with older women—on paper, I am talking about—for no matter how many lies one makes up about them, just to make them seem real and lifelike, some of them are sure to be true, or as near the truth as makes no matter. . . ."

And then, a good while later, when I had moved from Algiers to Lagouat, which is right away in the desert, hundreds of miles away in the desert, Ralph Trevor wrote to me, and among other things he asked: "Why haven't you mentioned Consuelo Brown in your last two letters? I am quite interested in her, and have been wondering whether you have fallen in love with her and had your advances rejected with contumely, which would be a quite sufficient reason for you to have lost all interest in her."

I wrote back rebuking him for his harsh opinion of me and pointing out various of the less lustrous episodes in his own career of celibacy, and then I came to Consuelo. "Yes, there is certainly a reason why I ceased to mention her in my letters, but it is not the reason to which you have quite bestially subscribed. There are some things one simply does not, of one's own accord, write about, not for any consideration, and so not even to cure you for ever of your fatuous pessimism concerning my character will I ever again mention the name of Consuelo Brown. I am, as you see, in Lagouat now, an aeroplane from Biskra dropped me here, and here I will stay until the spring, between the sand and the sun and the beggars. . . ."

But when in the spring I returned to London, loveliest of all towns in the spring, and I dined one night with Ralph Trevor, he said to me, at that period after dinner when such things are commonly said: "Now then, out with it, old man. The later history of Miss Consuelo Brown, if you please."

Very unwillingly, I told him how one day a young man I knew, not very well, was added to the guests of the hotel on the hill over the bay of Algiers. "A pleasant young man he was, and I was shocked at the sight of him, he was so white and fragile. He said he had been ill of a rheumatic fever for a long time and was now convalescing.

"We had met by chance on the very first day of his arrival, and we did the 'Hello! Fancy seeing *you* here!' business, but I fancied that his 'Hello!' was not so hearty as it might have been, considering that I was one of his elder brother's oldest friends. We sat down, on the terrace there, just before luncheon it was, and he seemed to be getting at something, until finally he came out with: 'Don't you know? Haven't you—haven't you heard?' I told him I hadn't seen an English paper for weeks, and then he sort of gasped out: 'Just the other day—in Paris—Basil—Basil shot himself! Awful, Oh, my God, awful!' Your own letter telling me of poor Basil's suicide was to arrive that very evening, so you can imagine how shocked I was to hear of the ghastly thing like that—and shocked too, at this poor boy's face, it was so livid with pain! I was so sorry for him that I was quite, quite silent. Here had he, at the end of a long illness, been running away from the turmoil of his elder brother's suicide—and the first man he meets is one of his brother's oldest friends! He had somehow had to tell me about it, the poor boy. And then there we sat, staring down at the silent Mediterranean a mile below, but the sea at noon was not more silent than we were. Not until that moment had I seen so clearly the wide, blue-white bay of Algiers, the sea as blue as a pretty doll's eyes and the bending coast dotted with white villages looking so deceptively clean in the sunlit distance, and away in the west, from the sea to the desert, the long low ridge of the Atlas Mountains with here and there snow-capped peaks towering up behind them, like huge white minarets in the blue haze of the sun . . . and then Consuelo came up the steps between us and the sea, pretty Consuelo, so slim, so young, so smart, and the poor boy beside me gasped 'My God!' Consuelo gave him one white look and was gone into the hotel, and that afternoon out of the hotel and, I hope to God, out of my life. Now, if you please, I am tired of this tale, and if you will be a little more active with that not very superior port, as becomes a host to his guest, I shall be infinitely obliged. Thank you."

"But, my dear man, you have not finished the tale! What the devil was it all about?"

"Yes, the devil and hell certainly had a lot to do with it, Ralph. There was hell in that poor boy's eyes when he saw Miss Brown and said 'My God!' You see, he loved that girl quite frantically and seriously, and she came to stay with him and his people in Hampshire so that the engagement could be confirmed and all that, and early one morning he saw her coming out of Basil's room. A hungry girl. After that he went away without a word, to give poor Basil his chance—you remember, we guessed that poor Basil was in love at last, the queer, furtive way he came by of breaking dinner-engagements?—and then the next thing he heard was that the girl had broken the engagement and that Basil had put a bullet into his silly sweet head. . . ."

"Perhaps," said Ralph Trevor, "she couldn't help it. Life is very hard for very pretty girls, Raymond. Perhaps she just couldn't help it. . . ."

But I said nothing, what was the use? I had seen that white look she gave that wretched boy, and that white look was like a disease in the sunlight. Lithe limbs and curling lips, laughing eyes and loose heart—a hungry girl, made to rot men.

# The Irreproachable Conduct of a Gentleman who once refused a Knighthood

## I

Said Mr. Fall to Lord Tarlyon on the telephone, one day in July:

"Pleased if you'd dine with me to-night."

"Sorry," said Lord Tarlyon; and he was sorry, for he liked Mr. Fall very well. "Promised to dine with a man."

"Pleased if you'd bring him along," said Mr. Fall.

Mr. Fall lived in Lord Brazie's house in Grosvenor Square. (Lord Brazie, of course, lived somewhere else, but he wouldn't have been able to live at all if Mr. Fall had not taken his house.) As George Tarlyon and I walked thither through the quietening streets and the dainty noises of the Town in the evening, we spoke of Cyrus Fall; and then a silence fell upon us, for we were meditating on millionaires of the Canadian sort. In the last decade of the last century millionaires were always American: in the first decade of this century an Australian mode set in, and many a young lady of birth was married to a fruit-farm, and many a chorus-girl decorated the bush: but fashion, as *The Tatler* has brilliantly put it, is proverbially fickle, and with the war all millionaires who were not Canadian fell into great discredit, so that many women exchanged theirs for the Canadian model on the first opportunity. Now of these, the greatest was Cyrus Fall. . . .

The history of Mr. Fall and his millions is simple. Like all Canadian millionaires he was born near Limerick and emigrated, with his parents, to Canada at the age of three. For a time he was dancing-master and chucker-out in a *cabaret* in Toronto; but, deciding that that was a discreditable profession, bought some newspapers and edited them in such an original way that he very soon became a Force. Throughout this time he never failed to consult his mother at every turn, and though in doing so he sometimes made mistakes, he never missed an opportunity of saying that a man's best friend is his mother; and when, at the age of thirty, having been a Force in Canada for some years, he came to England, he wrote to his mother, who of course lived in Winnipeg, every day, saying that a man should be grateful to the woman who gave him birth. In England Mr. Fall went on being a millionaire until the war broke out, when he at once became a multi-millionaire. He was offered a knighthood for his services on the field of finance, but humbly refused the honour in a letter which, his newspapers said, was that of a simple, sincere and great-hearted man and should be a historic model for all letters refusing knighthoods. Later on he refused a baronetcy in the same simple and sincere way, excusing himself to his friends on the grounds that his mother wouldn't like him making a guy of himself; and when some one said that Canadians can't be choosers Mr. Fall biffed him one. About the time when George Tarlyon and I were going to dine with him he was said to be about to accept a barony, excusing himself on the ground that he was getting too old for letter-writing. Mr. Fall had not married.

## II

I had never actually met Mr. Fall, but when we did meet he said he was pleased to know me, so that was all right.

"You will, of course, have a cocktail," he said.

"Of course," we said.

"My own particular make," Mr. Fall told us. "Instead of shaking them I stir them with a shagreen shoe-horn steeped in Chartreuse."

"Perfect it is," I assured him.

With the cocktails were caviare sandwiches.

"They go together very well," said George Tarlyon. When they had gone, we dined.

Somewhere near us, but not in the room, sang a *ukelele*: near enough to be enjoyed, far enough not to distract, a gentle noise, a mezzotint noise, unrecognisable and remote.

And then in the fullness of time, the table was cleared, and there was coffee.

"You will like the brandy," said Mr. Fall, as Tarlyon hesitated on the butler's question. We liked the brandy very much.

"Leave it," said Mr. Fall; and the butler left us.

"It's like this," he began; and he put both elbows on the table, and in one hand he waved a cigar and with the other he caressed his chin. Seriously he glanced from one to the other of us; he was a man with a courteous eye.

"It's like this," Mr. Fall addressed Tarlyon. "I asked you to dinner, Lord Tarlyon, not only because of the very real pleasure I take in your company, but because I want your advice—your advice," said Mr. Fall, "as an Englishman of honour. And for yours, too, Mr. Trevor, I shall be very much obliged. Have some brandy."

"You see," said Mr. Fall, "I am not a gentleman. I am not even quite a gentleman. My birth and upbringing, though they have fitted me for very much, have not fitted me to decide on certain matters with that clearness of vision and decision which I find so admirable in men of breeding. . . ."

Tarlyon made a faint noise which sounded like "Ah. . . ."

"To men like you," Mr. Fall continued, "there are not two ways of doing a thing: there is only a right way; and that, with you, is the instinctive way. Whereas for me there is also the right way, but there are other ways as well, and sometimes I find myself wandering up these other ways and wondering if they are not quite as right as the right way, even though they are more convenient. In matters of policy there are two sides to every question; and I sometimes wonder if, in matters of honour, there are not also two sides to every question. . . ."

"There are," said George Tarlyon. "But one of them is a precipice. . . ."

"Exactly, Lord Tarlyon. And that is why I am about to put before you the case of myself and a lady, as discreetly as possible of course, so that you can advise me what to do—as a man of honour. Or rather, so that you can support me in going on doing what I am already doing, or encourage me to change my course towards what, I frankly admit, will be a happy fulfilment for me. Have some brandy."

Mr. Fall, in the interests of his country at war, had frequently had occasion to voyage on board a cruiser of His Majesty's Fleet, and had thus acquired that finished courtesy which presumes a man has drunk nothing before the glass you are offering him.

"I may say," Mr. Fall continued, "that at the age of fifty-two I know as little about ladies as I did when I was twenty, when I didn't know any. Perhaps it is because I have always been a very busy man, perhaps it is because I do not attract them enough—"

"Or perhaps it's because you attract them too much," Tarlyon suggested.

"Of course," Mr. Fall admitted, "one is agreeable financially; and a knowledge of that fact has sometimes, I am afraid, caused me to reconsider an invitation to dinner which the night before had seemed full of friendship and, perhaps, possibilities of a kind which I am not too old to think romantic. However. . . ."

### III

"A little over a year ago," said Mr. Fall, "I met the lady who is bound up in the situation on which I need your advice. I met her in an ordinary way, at a ball; and saw nothing unusual in the meeting until the evening of the following day, when I found to my surprise that throughout the day she had been inhabiting that part of a man's mental economy which is called the 'back-of-his-mind.' On bringing her to the front I discovered that I was in love with her; and on ringing her up was delighted to hear that she was agreeably disposed to seeing me at her flat, at about five o'clock any afternoon. That was a year ago, and that is as far as I have got."

"You mean, she has so far refused to marry you?" I asked.

"I have not asked her, Mr. Trevor. That is the point—I cannot ask her. With such as she, as you can understand, the words love and marriage are synonymous—and both, to her in particular, are offensive. I am her friend. I do not want to be, but I am.

"She is a lady of birth, of deep principles and affections, which, I believe, it is the custom of the day to find wanting in women of fashion; and I find that, at the end of a year, I respect the dignity of her mind as much as I admire that of her carriage, her principles as much as her features, which are of the kind known as classical, though indeed I find in them every quality of romance. We were speaking, a moment ago, of ladies to whom a rich man is, if in no other way, financially agreeable. With this lady, that would suffice me: I would think myself well-rewarded to be allowed to marry her on any terms; but I would dare to offer her anything but the most trifling bric-a-brac—for not she to accept expensive presents—as little as I would dare to offer her my hand. I cannot even mention marriage to her, because of the damn silly thing which stands between us. Have some brandy.

"Her husband had died some twelve months before I met this lady, in Rome, where he was on political business, of a sudden chill. At that time I was also in Rome; and though I had never met his wife, or even knew he was married, I had had a fairly long acquaintance with him, which had begun in the early days of the war in Paris, where he was stationed as a military officer of some consequence. I remember he won the D.S.O. while I was there for service at the front—telephone service, I gathered.

"He died of his chill within twenty-four hours, and my business took me from Rome before his wife could arrive. I leave you to imagine the tragedy of her arrival in a city where, only a few years before, she had spent the happiest weeks of her life, her honeymoon, to look upon the still face of one who had left her two weeks before in the full vigour of youth and health. She has described it to me, not as a whole but in those disjointed pieces with which a sensitive mind can make a figure of tragedy vivid to a sympathetic listener, and I can see the thing so clearly that I feel it as a personal loss. . . ."

"And so," Mr. Fall added grimly, "it is. It seems that, on the night I met her at the ball, she had discovered my acquaintance with her dead husband; and it was that fact which had made her so agreeably disposed to allowing me to call on her, for hers was that kind of breeding—rare, I am given to understand, in these days—which is not usually approachable by a slight acquaintance on the telephone. I am quite assured, in spite of her very courteous assertions to the contrary, that we would never have become friends but for my having known her husband; and I, of course, was at first only too pleased to have chanced on a link which gave her a certain degree of pleasure in my person and company—for both, I have since discovered, were at first devoid of any other interest for her. Very early in our friendship I found that she had loved her husband as few men are fortunate enough to be loved; and in this love had been contained a respect which I can only describe as religious. It was not the qualities of his mind, which were gentlemanly but scarcely above the commonplace, but those of his heart, which had held such a high place in her love; and which, now that he was dead, reigned in her mind to the exclusion—I speak literally, Lord Tarlyon—of every other interest and affection. She had not loved him enough, she said. She ought, she insisted, to have recognised more deeply his regard for and constancy to her; and she ought certainly to have insisted on accompanying him to Rome when, perhaps, under her care, he might not have caught that fatal chill. She persuaded herself that she had neglected one whose every thought, whose whole life, was bound up in hers, a great gentleman whose fidelity to her, one of four daughters of an impoverished house, had merited the most utter devotion; and whose memory she couldn't but hold in the highest esteem, to the exclusion of every petty circumstance which might invade the life of a woman who was still young and, perhaps, not unattractive. Have some brandy.

"I need scarcely tell you, who are men of the world, that a lady so devoted, so consistent, is rare, and must undoubtedly possess qualities of mind and heart deserving a man's highest respect. Perhaps, however, I carried this respect business too far when, at that beginning, and in the natural flow of conversation about someone whose memory was so admirably dear to her, I helped to feed her illusion about her husband; but I was aware only of the present moment, and wished—and who, being human, would not?—to make myself agreeable enough for her to wish to see me again. For my success in that little intrigue I am now being sufficiently punished. In me, Mr. Trevor, and you, Lord Tarlyon, you may see at the present moment a man undergoing heavy punishment for the pettiest of all crimes, the crime of thoughtless kindness. I am now suffering for my lies, for I told more lies about that dead husband than you could believe possible in a man whose imagination has hitherto been considered financial rather than fanciful. I had, you understand, been so deeply impressed by her belief in the love and fidelity of her dead husband, had been so moved by the naïve illusions of a lady who, passing her life among a generation avid for the details of other people's infidelities, prized constancy above all things, that I had let myself go. It seemed, don't you see, the decent thing to do; and I, not being well versed in the rules concerning these matters, did it very thoroughly. Anyway, I could at best only have kept my mouth shut, for one breath of a hint adverse to that treasured memory would have snapped the slender cord of our friendship. But I need not, in trying to anchor her interest in me, have gone so far as I did: I need not, just for the pleasure of seeing the tender light in her eyes, have rashly struck out on my own and invented magnificent Parisian situations in which her husband's constancy to her had been as a shining light among the crude passions let loose by war among even the most decent of temporarily celibate men. I need not have depicted him as a man whose purity and asceticism was such as to astonish his friends—myself, who was but human, among them—and as one whom the fascinations of the most lovely women left untouched, except for a sad smile which I had frequently seen to come on his face, as at the thought of some one inexpressibly dear to him. Have some brandy.

"The man is dead; and I wouldn't have you think me so wanting in decency as to speak harshly of a dead man. But the fact remains that that man must have been one of the world's biggest liars, a liar of inconceivable genius and magnitude, a liar beside whom Ananias would have been a saint, Cagliostro a child, and Barry Lyndon a novice. As for Casanova, I simply hate to think how small he would have felt beside that dear, dead, faithful husband. I have told you how, throughout the time I knew him, I was not even aware that he was married; but there was not only nothing in his conversation, but there was less than nothing in his behaviour, to indicate that he had a wife in England for whose company he was passionately longing. I may say that I have never yet met a man who gave the appearance of passionately longing for his own wife less. I had nothing against him, mind you; he was a charming bachelor, a gay companion, and, if you will permit a small vulgarity, could resist a pretty woman about as much as a mouse can resist a cheese. He was certainly a shining light among the crude passions let loose by war; in fact, he shone magnificently; and a patriotic element in me was, in a dim kind of way, only too pleased to see him at it, for Frenchmen are nowadays so uppish about their talents at *le Sport*, what with one thing and another, that it was pleasant to see an Englishman learning them a thing or two about the one which, with boxing, they are most cocksure about. By the way, Lord Tarlyon, I wonder if you will agree with me when I suggest that this modern fashion among Englishwomen of decrying Englishmen as lovers in comparison to foreigners is not only getting very tedious but is, so I heard in a discussion on the matter with a student of my acquaintance, entirely without foundation in fact?"

"Our friend Trevor," said Tarlyon, with a sombre nod, "has been actively engaged in propaganda to that effect for some time: and with, I am told, no small measure of success."

"I am sincerely glad to hear that, Mr. Trevor; for it is by the accumulation of such small cancerous growths, perhaps scarcely significant in themselves but considerable in their rolling together, that the heart of an Empire is affected and its body grows rotten. The Dominion of Canada looks to you gentlemen of England to combat such insidious errors, which may seem harmless enough as part of the merry prattle of young ladies, but are, I am persuaded, detrimental to our particular civilisation. However. . . ." Mr. Fall waved aside our particular civilisation for the time being, and lit another cigar. He continued:

"The fever which proved fatal to this amorous gentleman in Rome was caused by exposure to the treacherous chill of that city in the early hours of the morning when, I am told, even a strong man's vitality is at its lowest; and the contrast between a warm place and the cold streets towards a hotel is sometimes more than the human constitution will bear. It has been my part to have had to sit and listen to his praises by the hour, and at his name I have had to endure seeing tears spring to the eyes of a noble and beautiful lady. With her I have stood by his grave, and on it I have emptied the contents of Solomon's windows. I have sat close beside her, and longed to touch her hand, to kiss her hair, to express even the surface of my passion—I have known that, perhaps, in happier circumstances, she might not have pushed away my hand nor denied my kiss—and I have also known that she would not allow herself for one second to deviate from the path she had set herself, the path of self-sacrifice to the memory of a man who, I knew, had never spent a moment of his life in thinking about her. Have some brandy.

"It may seem strange to you, Lord Tarlyon, and to you, Mr. Trevor, that I should confide in you with so little restraint. But, as I told you in throwing myself upon your kind attention, I lack the breeding which could alone give me an instinctive direction in such a matter. I need guidance, Lord Tarlyon. I am in a damnable case; and in the last few weeks I have been seeking refuge from a position which becomes more insupportable every moment—and the more so, you understand, because I can see I am not altogether distasteful to the lady—in wondering whether, in some recess in the code of honour, there is no decent way out of this damnable lie. That in particular is why, Lord Tarlyon, I was so anxious to see you, and to put the matter before you. Is there, for a man of honour, no way out of a mess like this? Is it utterly impossible for me to shatter her illusions about her late—her extremely late, in his nightly habits—husband? Is there nothing I can do but look sulky every time the man's name is mentioned? But I have tried that, and I am afraid she takes it as the expression of a sympathy too deep for words. What can I do, Lord Tarlyon? Or perhaps you, Mr. Trevor, can suggest some way out? Have some brandy."

A silence fell on us a while. At last I said:

"I'm afraid, Mr. Fall, as you have honoured me by asking for my advice, that there seems to be nothing you *can* do but what you have already done—to wait. Maybe sometime . . . she . . . well, you know what I mean." I hope he did, for I was by no means sure. . . .

"And you, Lord Tarlyon?"

"Well," said George, very thoughtfully, with his eyes somewhere on the table, "as you ask me, I must say that your behaviour throughout seems to me to have been irreproachable, and I respect you enormously for it. I can't say fairer than that. But," and he looked across at Mr. Fall; and he smiled at him a grave smile, "neither can I for the life of me see how you can break away from the position you are in. It seems beastly—but, since you've asked my advice, I can only suggest that you must just wait. You can't, as you have said, shatter the illusion—you can't, as a man of honour. A cad, of course, would long ago have stepped into the breach and away with the body—I mean, booty. Your brandy is marvellous, Mr. Fall. But, as I was saying, I can't for the life of me see that you can do anything but just wait and look sulky whenever you get the chance. . . ."

"You will forgive my boring you?" Mr. Fall put to us sincerely.

"It would be too cold-blooded of us to say we have been entertained," I began—

"But," said Tarlyon, "we have certainly not been bored. And I only wish we could have been of some use—"

"I just wanted cor-rob-or-ation," Mr. Fall murmured softly, sadly. "Have some brandy."

## IV

It was past one o'clock when George Tarlyon and I set foot again in Grosvenor Square; we walked up South Audley Street, and I stopped at my door.

"Good-night, George," I said. But Tarlyon held my arm.

"You are coming home with me," says he.

"Nonsense!" said I; and though I was friendly, I was firm. "There was once a woman in a play by Shaw who amazed five continents by the magic words 'Not bloody likely.' At this moment I am that woman, and it is thus that I refuse your solicitations. I have drunk brandy, and I would sleep. Good-night, George Almeric St. George."

But he is a very tall man, and he dragged me by the arm down South Audley Street, the while crying mighty cries after the manner of one who wants a taxi immediately; and into one he threw me, and the taxi hurled itself towards Belgrave Square, where George Tarlyon lives in a house which, together with much money, was left to him by his wife, who died before she could make a will.

I was very angry, and insisted that he should make a note of it.

"There, there," he soothed me. "All I want you to do, Ralph, is to leer in the offing while I ring up a lady. I do so hate to do that kind of thing alone."

I pointed out that she couldn't be much of a lady if he could ring her up at that unearthly hour, he warned me to leave his friends alone, I said I wouldn't touch them at the end of a barge-pole, and then I composed myself to sleep. The taxi hurled itself across Hyde Park Corner, and dreamily I heard Tarlyon's voice:

"I am not only going to telephone a lady, but I am going to insult a lady intolerably. And in case my invention should run low, I want you, Ralph, to stand by and suggest some more intolerable insults. . . ."

And dreamily I heard Tarlyon's voice:

"She keeps her telephone beside her bed, and so she must answer; and lo! I will insult her intolerably."

The taxi stopped, and very soon the receiver was to his ear, while I leered at him from the depths of an arm-chair.

"Have some brandy," said Tarlyon, but I sneered at him.

But what he said down the telephone, I cannot repeat. These things should only be spoken of privately, as between man and man. All I can do is to give a brief outline of his speech and a summary of the conclusions at which he arrived. He spoke at length of her character, of which he seemed to take an unfavourable view; he took grave exception to the manner of her life; and he begged her to hold him excused, in future, from any closer relationship than that of a distant acquaintance. She must have said he was drunk, for he denied any undue excess, while reserving to himself the right to think she was probably a secret drinker.

He began, I thought, rather subtly: on a matter which has been discussed between ladies and gentlemen ever since Solomon took a fancy to the Queen of Sheba and put off all dinner engagements for a week. In the gentlest way Tarlyon begged to be excused from dining with her on the following night. No, it was not that he had discovered a previous engagement; no, he couldn't say that. The truth was, he said, that he had found something better to do; he hadn't, he added, had to look very hard. He then proceeded to give his reasons for never wishing to see her again, and these he deduced (*a*) from flaws in her character, (*b*) from fissures in her temperament, and (*c*) from structural errors in her personal appearance. He pointed out that he was putting himself to this trouble only for her good, and in memory of his long friendship with her late husband, whom he had known ever since they were at Oxford and Cambridge together. I can only put down the fact that she did not ring off before she did to some fatal fascination in his voice, which was throughout smooth and reasonable in tone.

"That woman," he explained, "is a very clever woman. She has the kind of brains that don't generally go with beauty; and if I had any political ambitions, or any indoor ambitions of any kind, I would marry her like a shot. She has been thinking this last year that I might marry her, but I've just managed to keep the conversation off that. For, though one doesn't deserve an angel, one needn't marry a devil. Meanwhile, however, I've grown fond of her, and I've taken no trouble to hide from her that I admire her enormously; and so she has kept me dangling for a year, doing neither one thing or the other—indeed, why should she?—on the off-chance that I might marry her; for though Viscounts are not what they were, Ralph, a wealthy Viscount was to her mind just preferable to a wealthy Canadian of a certain age. And so she has kept poor old Cyrus Fall, who adores her, as I've known for the last ten months or so, hanging on as her second string, palming off that ghastly lie on him about a husband she never cared a damn about—she's just kept him hanging on, while she waited to see whether I'd toe the line or not; and if not . . . But I'm rather sorry about it all, Ralph, for she is a clever and amusing woman, and I shall miss begging her to put off Mr. Fall to dine with me."

"Poor old Cyrus Fall!" I murmured. "But then—why poor? He adores the woman—no matter how cunning she is, he adores her. And so on. . . ."

"Exactly," said Tarlyon. "There are men, Ralph, who would warn Mr. Fall against that woman, whereas we are throwing her into his arms. For we, Ralph, know that no matter how thoroughly he finds her out, as he surely will, he will not cease to adore her; for it is not virtue that men and women love in each other—"

"Quite," said I, "Good-night."

## V

A week later, there was announced in the *Morning Post*, which somehow always seems to know about these things, the engagement of Mr. Cyrus Fall to Mrs. Leycester-Craven, widow of Major Leycester-Craven of the—. The same morning Mr. Fall rang up Lord Tarlyon.

"Pleased if you'd take luncheon with me to-day," said Mr. Fall.

"Sorry," said Tarlyon. "Already luncheoning."

"Cocktail?"

"Well, why not?"

"Ritz, one o'clock?"

"Right," said Tarlyon.

Tarlyon grasped the outstretched hand, and wrung it.

"Congratulations," he murmured.

"Thank *you*," said Mr. Fall.

Tarlyon raised his eyebrows.

"But is the man mad?" he asked. "What on earth for?"

"For your advice to the lady, Lord Tarlyon," said Mr. Fall gently.

Tarlyon jumped in his chair, and he stared at Cyrus Fall.

"You don't mean to tell me that she told you!" he gasped.

"Oh, no!" Mr. Fall assured him. "Oh, no! She has never mentioned your name, and I haven't the faintest idea of what you said to her. But I knew that you would say something, Lord Tarlyon—as a man of honour. That is why I told you of my dilemma that night—after which, as a man of honour, you could do but one thing, since my intentions were serious and yours were not. A cocktail?"

"I'll have some brandy," whispered Tarlyon.

# Salute the Cavalier

## I

The Felix Waites, as every one knows, are the most exclusive people in Hampstead. And since the war, with its attendant new people, the family have become so aristocratic that they can scarcely speak, for Mrs. Felix Waite says that every one talks too much nowadays. The Felix Waites are understood to spend most of their time in the country, where they entertain only very small parties. There was a time when they spent anxious moments about their only son, Thomas, but all that is over now. Once upon a time young Thomas did the superman on them about a chorus-girl, and broke away. Young Thomas had never fancied himself as an aristocrat, and so he did not marry the chorusgirl at once; but he said he would, and in the meanwhile he concentrated on making money. He was understood to be making big money—so big that he could inhabit a suite of rooms at the Ritz for a week, sign the bill in pencil, and get away before the hotel clerks had rubbed the dazzle of his sapphire tie-pin out of their eyes. But one day young Thomas forgot to wear his tie-pin, whereupon he adjourned to Brixton Prison for two days and four hours, which he spent in trying to imagine the expression on his father's face on hearing of his son's latest telegraphic address. However, Mr. Felix Waite paid up like a gentleman, as he did everything else like a gentleman. That is the only time a Felix Waite has ever stayed with King George, but they do not mention it. Whether the chorus-girl became a footlight-favourite or just faded away was never known. Young Thomas married county.

It occurred to Mrs. Felix Waite during the season of 1922 that she might give a garden-party. There was a something about a garden-party, a certain elegance which, Mrs. Felix Waite thought, was lacking in a ball. Every one, after all, can give a ball. Whereas, except for the King and the Queen, very few can give a garden-party in London, for the central idea of a garden-party is that it be held in a garden, and gardens in London are rarer than the jewels on the Mikado's brow. Now Mrs. Felix Waite had a spacious garden; and about it the walls were so high that the youth of Hampstead Heath had to stand on each other's shoulders to catch a glimpse of the garden life of the gentry.

## II

The garden-party was a great success. Quite half the people who were asked came, and nearly all the people who weren't. The fact that it poured with rain from three o'clock onwards might have interfered with the pleasure of the company, had not Mrs. Felix Waite been a woman of invention and, with great presence of mind, held the garden-party in her spacious drawing-rooms; thereby, some have thought, changing the garden-party into an At Home or Afternoon Reception, but that is a matter for argument.

Among those present was Mr. Michael Wagstaffe, the young gentleman with the broken nose who called himself, with perhaps too much pomp, the cavalier of the streets; a list of what other people called him might be of interest, but could have no bearing on this story. It was not a habit with the cavalier of the streets to go to garden-parties, or to parties of any kind, for in London there were not a few people who would have been pleased to meet him just once more. However, on this occasion, he had happened to be passing Mrs. Felix Waite's house towards six o'clock, and, hearing music and being thirsty, had walked in. Not long after, he walked out. But he had not walked more than a few yards when someone caught his shoulder, and an abrupt voice said:

"Come back, you!"

Mr. Michael Wagstaffe turned round. "I never drink with strangers," he said proudly.

"Come on, now," said the gruff man impatiently. "No one can leave that house just yet. And we want you particularly—to ask you a few questions."

"A detective!" sighed Mr. Wagstaffe. "I knew it! For his clothes are very plain."

They started back, the plain-clothes man holding his arm. It was still raining hard—one of those afternoons when people paid to watch it rain on a nice new tarpaulin at the new tennis-courts at Wimbledon.

"I return under protest," said Mr. Wagstaffe, "though I wouldn't object to an umbrella as well."

"We know *you*," the plain-clothes man grinned disagreeably. "We know *you*. And I've had my eye on you in there—you weren't invited, you weren't."

They walked up the soaked red strip of carpet into the spacious portico, through the spacious portico into the spacious Lounge Hall, and so into a little room. The garden-party, it seemed, was still in full swing in the drawing-rooms; there was music, there was gaiety, but in the little room downstairs were only the plain-clothes man and the cavalier of the streets. Methodically, the plainclothes man began to search the cavalier's pockets. Contentedly, the cavalier let him.

"If it's cigarette-cards for your children you're looking for," he said, "I'm afraid I left my collection at home. And if it's not cigarette-cards, what the hell *are* you looking for?"

"Diamonds," said the detective. "Off with your shoes now."

"I always was a devil for diamonds. Whose diamond?"

"Lady of the house lost famous diamond-ring. Come on now, off with your shoes."

"If you are worthy enough to untie them," grinned Mr. Wagstaffe, and held out a wet and rather muddy shoe. But there were no diamond rings in Mr. Wagstaffe's shoes.

"Good-bye," said Mr. Wagstaffe amiably.

"*Au revoir*," the detective grinned. He was annoyed. "You'll see more of me, *Mr.* Wagstaffe. Call on you soon, perhaps."

The young man turned round at the door.

"Going to search all the guests?" he asked.

"'Course not. But you had no right in the house. You was loitering suspiciously."

"Going to search the other people who came unasked?" asked Mr. Wagstaffe gently.

"Don't pull any of that on me, young man," said the plain-clothes man. "You was the suspicious character on the premises when the diamond-ring was stolen, and you'll hear more of it."

The cavalier of the streets advanced gently upon the plain-clothes man, and gently he smiled upon him.

"If you knew more of your London," said he, "you would know that there were at least five other suspicious characters in this house, of whom not more than two could have been invited. And the next time you come near me you had better bring a posse along with you for protection, for at one more word from you I will smite you in such a manner that if you don't fall down instantly I shall have to run behind you to see what's holding you up. Good-afternoon."

As Mr. Wagstaffe emerged from the little room into the spacious hall a young lady passed him towards the door. She passed swiftly, intently, and sweetly, for she was a pretty young lady. She was dressed like a flower, a flower from a garden sweeter than the spacious garden of Mrs. Waite, and as she passed by the cavalier of the streets a faint scent pierced the rain-sodden air of the outer hall.

"Chypre," thought Mr. Wagstaffe, for it was his business to know these things.

"Good-afternoon," said Mr. Wagstaffe amiably; but the young lady, the very smart young lady, passed him without a glance into a waiting taxi-cab outside.

The cavalier of the streets whistled gently as he walked away in the rain. He walked not because he liked walking, but because he had not the price of a taxi in the world, because the Underground was offensive to his sensitive nerves, and because buses bored him.

### III

In an obscure but not unclean street towards the northern fringe of Soho there is to be found by the seeker after experience a restaurant, where gentlemen in Mr. Wagstaffe's predicament may dine very passably; and, on having inscribed the bill with their temporarily worthless signatures, pay on some happier day. Very seldom, indeed, had the cavalier of the streets actually fallen to this pass; these were his most unfortunate days; and not even a bottle of the Rhine wine for which M. Stutz was famous—for such was the name of the polite and amiable *patron* of the Mont Agel Restaurant—was, on this evening, able to support him in the sardonic optimism with which he had always parried the most cruel thrusts of a vagabond destiny.

Than the year 1922 there has never been a more dolorous year for gentlemen of enterprise, as instance the luckless experiences of Mr. Gerald Lee Bevan and Mr. Bottomley; and though the cavalier of the streets was not only a gentleman of enterprise but also of imagination, even he could not imagine money where money was not. Whereat he was depressed.

But money, though naturally of the first importance in an adventurous life, was not the immediate cause of Mr. Wagstaffe's depression as he dallied with a morsel of caviare and a piece of toast *Melba*. A face haunted his memory. A lovely face it was, mature and gracious and remote—Ah, from him how remote! This face (and with it gray eyes, witty and understanding eyes) had happened to him in the course of a most unfortunate episode some months ago. He would never see her again—or, rather, she would never see him. She would look through him, the cavalier of the streets who had blackmailed her and then repented of his sin because of the beauty of her face and the bravery of her voice. But he would certainly see her, as an outcast in a wilderness may, through the leaves and tree-trunks of his prison, just glimpse a brilliant figure in a noble pageant; for the face that haunted him was of the world, and, in these days of many illustrated journals, had acquired an international reputation as one of the five leading faces of Europe. Thus, it had come to pass that the cavalier of the streets, meshed in a hopeless admiration, nowadays found little pleasure in his way of life; nor did the pursuit and beguiling of Mugs, which had been his source of income and entertainment ever since he had acquired a taste for it at the University of Oxford, any longer divert him. The face of his lady love, ever haunting his memory, deprived him of his wonted pleasure in living dangerously. Whereat he was depressed.

"I must leave England," he thought. "I must go to some foreign city and lead a quite different life. But to leave England requires money; and to lead a quite different life also requires money." He came to a sudden decision; made the gesture of payment upon the bill, and, thanking the courtly M. Stutz, left the restaurant, and walked swiftly westwards through the twilight of the streets.

## IV

Indifferent to all about him, the young man strode on his way through the festive crowds that only the most inclement weather can prevent from promenading Oxford Street on a night in June. He saw nothing, he heard nothing; he was in a great hurry; and it was only as his determined steps were brought almost to a standstill by the great concourse of people about Oxford Circus that his eyes found leisure to examine the placards of the evening journals which were exhibited at the mouth of the Tube Station. "Countess Divorces Husband." Well, thought he, she couldn't very well divorce her brother, could she? "Famous Diamond Stolen." Ah! "Garden Party Thief." "£2000 Ring Stolen at Society Function." "Society Hostess Robbed." It's almost worth it for her, he thought cattishly, to be called a Society Hostess. And he grinned, and, assuming a fierce expression, which it was not difficult for him to do under the angle of his dilapidated felt hat, he parted the crowds about him and went his way. Maybe it was that the placards had had a stimulating effect on him, or maybe it was that he needed violent exercise, but now he walked even more swiftly than before, oblivious of the remarks which his arrogant passage aroused from the leisurely promenaders.

Soon he turned into a quiet street, and from that into another; and came at last to a large building which, despite the name of Lyonesse Mansions, was a block of flats of the meaner sort. He entered and strode up and up, until the genteel strip of carpet on the stairway gave up all pretence of being a genteel strip of carpet and frankly became a drugget of the consistency of a Gruyère cheese.

To the very top of Lyonesse Mansions strode the cavalier of the streets, and when further progress was barred by a mean-looking door he banged upon that door without restraint, once, twice, thrice; and was then opposed by a feminine person who had all the attributes and mannerisms of a Slut, but was in reality a respectable woman with a vote, the wife of a chauffeur who lived in a neighbouring Mews and whose comforts she increased by doing a bit of charing here and there. She was doing a bit of it here at the moment, and seemed inclined to resent any interruption on behalf of both herself and her employer, for before he had said a word she had snapped "Out," and only the dexterous shoe of the cavalier of the streets prevented the door from being slammed in his face.

"You'll get a sore throat if you snarl like that," he advised her kindly, and pushed past her into the narrow little hall. Thoughtfully, he looked at the three closed doors with which the narrow little hall was decorated; and, by the abstracted expression of his face, seemed to be in a place far removed from the comments on his manners, appearance, and antecedents, if any, which the char-lady, having left the open doorway, poured into his ear.

Then, having thought out his thought, he strode to the middle door and flung it open. The room was dimly lit, which was just as well, for there was in it but one ornament which might have repaid a more exact scrutiny; and that was a girl, who, dressed for solitude in a faded blue *peignoir*, her fair hair loose about her shoulders, a copy of the *Sketch* in her hands, lay negligently on a wretched sofa. She was a pretty girl; that has been remarked before; but then she had been dressed like a flower, a flower from a garden sweeter than the spacious garden of Mrs. Felix Waite, and now she was dressed like nothing at all; and the faded blue of her covering was stained by a flat yellow packet of cigarettes. She was obviously no lady, and had given up pretending she was.

"You dirty beast! How dare you come here!" cried the pretty girl, amazement turning to disgust, disgust to anger. But the cavalier of the streets, still framed in the doorway, his head uncovered, only smiled at her. And in his smile there was no hint of apology for the intrusion which his hostess seemed to resent so deeply.

"Good-evening, Betty," said he, in a friendly way. "Just thought I'd come and look at you, you know. Pretty Betty! You last remarkably well, I must say. How are you, child?" And he advanced into the room, threw his hat on a chair, dug his hands into his pockets, and grinned at her again; while her eyes, pretty blue eyes hardened by despair, stared up at him in helpless anger.

"Michael," she said bitterly, "you are the world's worst man. Why can't you leave me alone?—my Gawd, why can't you leave me alone?" And as her voice rose, her eyes swept him in utter contempt.

"You poor kid, I *have* left you alone," he told her gently, wearily. The fact that the cavalier of the streets had at one time been a gentleman was apparent in the way he took abuse. Abuse made him tired. "I haven't been near you for years, Betty, so it's no good your handing me any rough stuff about *that*. . . ."

His gentleness provoked her. The pretty girl sat up in her disorder, and the expression on her face was not pretty. He smiled curiously, thinking of a very young man up at Magdalen College and of a very pretty girl at a flower-shop near the station, and how the young man had loved the pretty girl from a distance, until one day he had realised that the pretty girl was very willing to be loved by him; whereupon she had got the sack from the flower-shop, and had come up to London for to be a chorus-girl, and in due course the young man had forgotten her. . . .

"Anyway," he added, "I didn't leave you so stranded as that Thomas Felix Waite fellow."

Shame that the blue of the pretty girl's eyes was so hard, so wretched and so hard. "Oh, yes," she sneered; "there ain't much to choose between you two rotten gentlemen!" And she laughed; and then, because she was a girl, she sobbed. "Oh, Christ, why've I always been so wretched!"

He was silent for what seemed a long time. Her sobs spent themselves quietly in the depths of her self-pity, and at last he said softly: "Anyway, Betty, you've got your own back on the Felix Waite family now. You'll be able to go back to the country, as you've always wanted to, and live comfortably for a time. Or perhaps you'll be able to start a little shop of some kind."

She stared at him in immense amazement, but he was looking out of the little window. . . .

"Michael Wagstaffe," she breathed, "what the blazes are you talking about?"

"A diamond ring worth £2000," said Michael Wagstaffe to the window.

"Balmy!" she jeered at him.

"Hand it over, Betty," said the cavalier of the streets sharply. He stared down her frightened, incredulous look. "It's no good your saying you haven't got it, because I guessed you had when I saw you leaving the Felix Waite house this evening, and I *know* you have now I've seen your face. . . ." She began shrilly, but he snapped her up. "Now don't be silly, child. It's no good your being selfish with it because you'll never be able to get rid of it on your own, and you'll only get copped if you try. I know about these things. So hand it over and try not to look as though I was boring you with a tale about potatoes sprouting from the Albert Memorial. We'll go halves on it, I'm telling you. But you'll have to trust me."

She leapt up, faced him, a figure of tense fury. "I trust *you*! You poor silly cad, I trust *you*! Get away from my sight before—" And she suddenly realised that she had not denied having the diamond-ring, that he had provoked her outburst, that he was laughing at her. She threw herself down on the sofa again and fumbled in the yellow packet for a cigarette.

"Clever, aren't you!" she sneered.

"Only by contrast," smiled the cavalier of the streets. "I shall have to find it myself, then?"

She made a move as though to spring from the sofa, but it was only a little move, for she knew her man, and he was standing just beside her. "You're just a blamed fool," was all she said.

"Don't move, Betty," he begged her gently. "Please don't move. Because I don't want to have to tie you up. All I want to do is to find that diamond-ring. It's silly of you to put me to the trouble of having to look for it, but even so I shall give you half of whatever I get for it, for which you must thank my late mother for the way she brought me up." He seemed to have fallen into a conversational vein; he heeded not the contemptuous sounds with which the pretty girl—now, alas! not so pretty as she had been—sought to disturb the even tenor of his conversation; and all the while his eyes were busy about the room, a largish and dingy bed-sitting-room, the bed being inadequately hidden in an alcove behind a frayed green curtain.

"You see, Betty dear," he went on, "I have come to a point in my life when I must have money or bust. I am telling you this that you may know I shall not spend half your ill-gotten gains in riotous living. I am tired of riotous living, Betty. I am tired of my life, I am tired of England. And so I am going abroad, far abroad, and there I shall make a new start—" She tried frantically to jump up, but he caught her wrist and held it— "make a new start, as I was saying. You will not see me again for a long time, Betty, and when you do, you will see a rich and generous man, for I shall never forget that I owe you a good turn for the wrong I did you. But to go abroad and to begin an entirely new life I need money. And so," and his eyes still wandered thoughtfully about the room, "I must find your diamond-ring, sell it for you, and keep half the proceeds as commission. . . ."

"Even if it was here," jeered the pretty girl, "you'd never find it. You think you're the only clever one in the world, don't you?" But there was not much conviction in her voice.

"No, I've always said you had brains, Betty. You are no fool; and I shall conduct my investigations on those premises. But don't move—" and his hand fell sharply on her wrist again, while his eyes still thoughtfully embraced every corner of the room. "Now, if you were a fool, where would you hide a stolen diamond-ring so that your maid would not find it? You would hide it in a far corner of a drawer, or under a pile of linen, or you would sew it into the lining of a dress, or bury it in a hole in the floor—in fact, Betty dear, if you were a fool you would hide that diamond-ring in some secret place which any charwoman or detective searching this room would find at once. But you are not a fool. Now, if you are a student of Edgar Allen Poe, which I doubt, you will remember his tale about a young Frenchman called Duval, or Dupin, I forget which, who found a purloined letter, after the Paris police had searched in vain for it for weeks, in the most obvious place in the robber's house: which was, of course, the letter-rack. Now what, I ask myself, is the most obvious place in this room in which to hide a stolen diamond-ring? The answer at once leaps to my mind, my eyes wander to a dilapidated-looking arm-chair a few yards away and fix on a hand-bag which is lying in the seat thereof. It is a pretty hand-bag, unpretentious but decorative; and a diamond-ring in your hand-bag would be quite safe from the prying fingers of your maid or charwoman for the simple reason that she has long ago given up hoping that she will find any money in it. But I am neither your maid nor your charwoman, and—Oh!" She had bitten the hand that held her wrist, and only by a very quick effort did he restrain her from reaching the arm-chair on which lay the hand-bag. "Allow me," he said politely, nursing his hand. "I will get it for you." Swiftly he got it—and the diamond-ring lay in his open palm.

All fight had left the pretty girl; she sat listlessly on the sofa and gave way to her misery.

"Oh, you beast, you beast!" she kept whispering between dry sobs.

The cavalier of the streets stared at the stone in his hand. It winked and glittered, a bright white light on a dingy palm in a dingy room, arrogantly daring the eye with its innumerable carats. He whistled softly, in wonder. "And they say," he murmured, "that diamonds aren't fashionable nowadays!"

From the diamond in his palm he looked at the bowed head of the girl. He said harshly:

"Haven't I told you I'm going to give you half of what I get?"

"I don't want to sell it," sobbed the girl. "I got reasons. You wouldn't understand—*you* wouldn't understand anything to do with sentiment. You was born without a heart, Michael Wagstaffe. When young Thomas Felix Waite loved me he promised me that he'd get that diamond-ring from his mother and give it to me. I didn't want it then, nor believe him, but he went on so about it that I came to fix my mind on it. And then one day he left me—just like that, without a word. He was a weak idiot, but I loved him—*you* wouldn't understand. And when he left me my mind somehow ran on that diamond-ring he'd promised me—I wanted it, d'you see, as I might want some money that's owing to me. God's treated me pretty rough, I thought, and so He owes me that diamond-ring just so as I can look at it now and then. And I been thinking about it months and months, not thinking to steal it, you know, but just wanting it. *You* wouldn't understand how soft a girl gets when she's eaten up with loneliness in a big place like London. Why didn't you let me be at Oxford, Michael, living with my father? And so when I saw this garden-party billed in the Society columns this morning, I just thought I'd try to get in and have a look at the diamond on her hand. I never thought she'd be fool enough to take it off in that catch-as-catch-can crowd to show to a friend, and then lay it on the edge of the fight-for-a-cup-of-tea-table to grab a cake which she could have done well without, she being already so fat with overfeeding. . . ." And for the first time she looked up at the young man, who stood above her absently playing with the glittering toy in his hand. She stared at him with babyish, unbelieving eyes. "Gawd, you're a bad kind of man, Michael Wagstaffe. You're very bad."

"You don't want to sell it, then?" he asked sardonically.

"I want the diamond—my diamond!" she whispered. "Give me back my diamond-ring, Michael Wagstaffe. It'll do for the sun you've took from me since we met at Oxford. . . ."

He smiled at her suddenly. "Here you are, pretty Betty," he said, and held out the diamond.

But Betty was afraid; she didn't believe the *beau geste*. Few *beaux gestes* had come pretty Betty's way. "Don't play with me," she whispered.

"Go on, take the damn thing. I'll swim the Channel." There was no doubt about it now. She stretched out her hand to his, to the glittering thing in his palm; but her hand never reached the glittering thing. He followed her staring, terrified eyes to the door behind him.

"Evening, *Mr.* Wagstaffe," said the plain-clothes man with a grin; and he fixed a delighted eye on the glittering thing in the palm of Mr. Wagstaffe's hand. "How's business with diamonds tonight?"

"Rotten," said Mr. Wagstaffe slowly. "Girl's afraid even to touch it."

The plain-clothes man was delighted with himself; he didn't hurry; he turned to the two constables who filled the doorway behind him. "See, boys! There's not a thief in the world who won't take a stolen jool to show off to his best girl. That's why I've kept you chasing this smart young man all evening—I knew he had it, but I wanted to catch him *in flagrante derelicto*, which is Latin for making a fool of himself." He possessed himself of the ring from the young man's hand. "Sorry to have disturbed you, miss. I didn't like doing it, but he was such a long time in here, and he's given us the go-by so often, that I thought I'd come up and fetch him, as he and I are going the same way home to-night. Come on, *Mr.* Wagstaffe."

The pretty girl, who had sat like a numbed thing, stirred violently; she opened her mouth: "But—"

"I'm glad," said the cavalier sharply, "to see that you took my advice about bringing a posse with you. I'm coming."

"But I—" began Betty, incredulously, desperately.

"That's all right, miss," the detective soothed her. "He won't be any more trouble to you for sixteen months or so."

"Look here, I took—" began Betty furiously, as they moved to the door.

"Good-night, pretty Betty," called the cavalier of the streets. "I'm sorry about the wrong I did you at Oxford. But I'll do you a good turn one day. . . ."

Betty rushed frantically towards them, but the detective slammed the door in her face; and through the flimsy panels she heard the gay voice of the cavalier of the streets:

"Come, gentlemen, remove the body."

# The Shameless Behaviour of a Lord[1]

## I

This is quite a simple story, but it is about a lord. The lord in question was John Tiberius Vincent de Guy, second Viscount Paramour, and he was wealthy beyond the dreams of avarice. He was, in fact, so wealthy that Mr. Otto Kahn stood at attention when speaking to him and Mr. John D. Rockefeller burnt his tongue with his hot milk at the mere mention of his name. Of course, young Lord Paramour had not made the money himself; he merely decorated it. His father, the late Watt A. Guy, will be remembered as the inventor and promoter of the Paramour Safety Hairpin: which, it has been said, has made a deeper impress on contemporary life than any other invention except Beecham's Pills. It was thought pretty decent of the old man that, when one day as he lay on his death-bed the Prime Minister dropped in to hand him a Viscounty, he instantly took as his title the name which had made his millions, and died Lord Paramour; in which choice some people of the meaner sort have professed to find a particular aptness, for had not (they asked) the most famous advertisement of the Hairpins, that one which has for more than a decade been emblazoned in coloured lights across the eastern end of Piccadilly Circus and has raised advertisement to the majesty of

---

[1] With apologies to, I believe, Catulle Mendès, but I am not sure, for I have not read his works. I would like to, but my French is limited. On the publication of this tale in a journal, a friend told me that the idea had already been used by Catulle Mendès: but I have retained it, I am not sure why.

an institution—had not those letters of fire beseeched: " Buy Paramour, Lord of Hairpins. No Woman Should be Without"? Whereupon, to be sure, no woman was.

Of young Lord Paramour it must be said that he was a gentleman of spirit; the war found him no laggard; but he was not ambitious in the arts of peace. It pained some of his most worthy friends to see with what indomitable energy he pursued the professions of leisure and luxury; that he used his immense fortune and unusual parts—which it has always been the pleasure of worthy persons to discern in the immensely rich—to no other advantage than the decorations of his various palaces and castles, the lavish entertainment of his friends therein, and only the most unthinking exercise of charity; but those nearest to him were most of all displeased at his evasion of his duty to his line and to society, for young Lord Paramour showed a strong disinclination to marry. A pageant of young ladies of quality was passed before him in review, but he either heeded them not or remarked, in a most amiable manner, on the imperfections of line, carriage, and cosmetics which (he said) were apparent in the most recent generation of young ladies. There were not, of course, wanting a few ladies of determination to make a formidable attack on his celibacy on behalf of their daughters; but young Lord Paramour withstood them with what can only be called a humiliating ease.

## II

The Albert Hall Ball, in aid of the Hospitals of London, will be remembered by many people as one of the most brilliant entertainments of the brilliant season of 1922. But it will be remembered by Mrs. Lyon-West—she was a New York Lyon before she married a Hampshire West—for a remarkable conversation with young Lord Paramour, who, after dancing with her beautiful daughter, had drifted into her box. The word "drifted" is here used in its strictly nautical sense, for Lord

Paramour had not the faintest idea into whose box he was entering. He had, after having danced with Miss Lyon-West (whose name he did not know, which is a grave reflection on the present state of society) discovered a distaste for the company of his guests in his own box, and had wandered to the first door he saw and shoved it open. Lord Paramour was an abstemious young man, but that night he had indulged in a glass or so of wine, wittily remarking to a friend that "a chap can't dance in cold blood."

"Why, good-evening, Lord Paramour!" cried Mrs. Lyon-West brightly.

"Ah," said Lord Paramour. "'Evening. Sorry, I'm sure." And he proceeded to drift out of the box again.

"But please don't go so soon, Lord Paramour! I am *delighted* to see you. Only a moment ago I was remarking how *beautifully* you and my daughter were dancing together!"

"Your daughter? Ah!" And Lord Paramour, who couldn't for the life of him remember the lady's name, nor where he had met her, sat down and regarded her benevolently. "Better call her madam," he thought to himself.

"Enchanting girl, madam. Enchanting dancer. Enchanting lines. Enchanting everything. In fact, madam, a very adequate girl, your daughter."

"I am *so* glad you like her," said Mrs. Lyon-West brightly. Mrs. Lyon-West had a reputation to keep up as to brightness.

"Like her, madam!" cried Lord Paramour. "I like her enormously. Most girls, I find, are rather tiresome—but your daughter, madam, is most unusual. And she is witty, which is remarkable in a girl. Please don't deny it—I distinctly heard her say something witty while we were dancing. She said, if I remember aright: 'The art of dancing is not to dance but to avoid other dancers.' Now that, madam, is a *mot*, in fact it is a *bon mot*. I am very partial to a *bon mot*, madam. And considering that I had just bumped the back of her head into some ass's elbow I think it was very apt of her. I was much impressed by your daughter, madam."

"Of course," said Mrs. Lyon-West, "looks aren't everything. A woman should be clever as well as beautiful—"

"Exactly," said Lord Paramour. "Exactly. Or quite."

"She reads such a lot!" sighed Mrs. Lyon-West.

"Well, well, there's nothing like reading," said Lord Paramour. "Personally, I can never find anything to read these days. Lot of septic trash."

"But you are so fastidious, Lord Paramour!"

"Oh, not at the moment, madam!"

"Well, then, why are you so long getting married?" asked Mrs. Lyon-West with a bright smile.

"Lot of trash," again sighed Lord Paramour. "Young women very inferior these days, madam. Always, of course, excepting your daughter."

"Don't except her. Marry her," said Mrs. Lyon-West wittily.

"Not bad, that!" chuckled Lord Paramour. "But not good, either. Would she, d'you think, consider my advances favourably?"

Mrs. Lyon-West thought she would, and Lord Paramour sighed.

"Shall I tell you," he put to her, "something that I have never told any one else? Shall I tell you why I have never married and why I cannot marry your daughter, enchanting though she is? Are you sure you will not be offended?"

"Tell me," said Mrs. Lyon-West. "Oh, please tell me!" She had not dreamed of getting so far.

"Well, it's like this," began Lord Paramour sadly. "But I must put it delicately. If you have read or seen *Trilby*, you will remember that the three artist fellows were terribly upset on hearing that Trilby had sat to another artist fellow for the 'altogether.' You get my meaning, madam? You are not offended?"

Mrs. Lyon-West said she did and she wasn't.

"Well, then, it's like this. I am, madam, incapable, constitutionally, physically, and mentally incapable of marrying any one whom I have not seen in the 'altogether'—"

"Sir," said Mrs. Lyon-West, "how dare you?"

"That's just the point," sighed Lord Paramour. "I daren't. And that's why I can't marry any one." He rose, saying sadly: "I knew you would be offended. Women are odd. Good-night, madam. Sorry, I'm sure. Enchanting girl, your daughter. She has promised me this dance. Good-night, madam."

"Sir," said Mrs. Lyon-West, "good-night."

### III

Now a digression here on the attitude of worldly mothers to their daughters might be of interest, but would not further this story. Let it suffice, in the chronicle of the shameless behaviour of young Lord Paramour, to say that Mrs. Lyon-West was a mother after the Roman model, and exacted from her offspring no less than abject obedience in all matters which might obtain to her welfare; in which she was helped by the fact that her beautiful daughter, in the days following the Albert Hall Ball, showed a pleasing inclination for the company of the witty and elegant Lord Paramour. Whereupon Mrs. Lyon-West asked him down to the Lyon-West place for the week-end.

The omission of Mr. Lyon-West from this story may seem marked; and if we are going down there with Lord Paramour politeness demands a glance at him. Meet Mr. Lyon-West. He is a little gentleman with an amiable eye and a hard and soft tennis court on his head. He does not matter very much.

Among the other guests at the house-party, as they revealed themselves after dinner on Saturday night, were Lord Pro and Lady Con—who, as of course you know, is a Beaver in her own right. That amiable baronet, Sir Courtenay Langouste, sat in a secluded corner reading the 68th edition of *If Winter Comes*, while his lady near-by cut the pages of the 69th edition. Major

General Sir Auction Bridges was with Mr. Soda, hotly contesting Mr. Soda's theory that hiccups was an infectious disease and could be prevented by inoculation. Lady Savoury, our first female M.P. and a great Improver, went about from group to group, indignantly remarking that it served Oscar Wilde right if only for saying that work is the curse of our drinking classes. Mrs. Custard, on the other hand, retired early, complaining that she was very short of long gloves.

During a break in the conversation, which was witty and sustained, Lord Paramour was understood to say that he would not be going to divine service the next day; and his hostess was obliging enough to say that, in that case, she too would not go to the morning service, but would walk Lord Paramour round the grounds; which would, she said, repay an early morning visit. Miss Lyon-West was understood to say that she came to the country for rest.

As, next morning, the countryside sweetly echoed with the songs of birds and church-bells, Lord Paramour and his hostess stepped out of the house upon the velvet sward. The broad sweep of park and woodland lay before them, soft and mellow in the haze of the morning sun, and Lord Paramour suggested a brisk walk, but Mrs. Lyon-West begged to be excused, saying she was enamoured of her rose garden; in which direction, skirting the spacious house, they leisurely betook themselves, talking of this and that in an elegant way.

"Penelope," said Mrs. Lyon-West—for such was her daughter's name: "Penelope loves gardens. Especially rose gardens."

"Indeed," said Lord Paramour. "Well, there's nothing like a rose garden."

"*How* I agree with you!" said Mrs. Lyon-West brightly. "Penelope, however, carries it almost to an infatuation."

" 'Pon my word!" said Lord Paramour.

"Yes, Lord Paramour. During the rose season, for instance, she *insists* on occupying a suite on the ground floor, from which she can at any moment step out and bathe herself in the beauty of the flowers. . . ."

"You turn a phrase very prettily, madam."

"Oh, *thank* you, Lord Paramour," breathed Mrs. Lyon-West. "But, as you will understand, her occupying a bedroom and a bathroom just *there* makes things just a leetle awkward. For she *insists* on having her blinds drawn open, that she may enjoy the roses over her toilet, and so *of course* the gardeners cannot enter the rose garden during the morning, as it distracts them from their work."

"Lazy dogs!" cried Lord Paramour.

"Ah, here it is!" cried his hostess as, rounding an angle of the house, they came upon the rose garden. "It is supposed to be the best rose garden in the country."

"Enchanting," said Lord Paramour. "Enchanting, considering the gardeners do no work in it in the mornings."

"Oh, there's Niblick, the agent!" cried Mrs. Lyon-West. "I *must* speak to him for a moment. Do excuse me a moment, Lord Paramour. I will be back in *one* moment."

Lord Paramour, of course, excused her; and very pleasantly whiled away twenty minutes with a cigarette in the rose garden. He paced about . . . He saw the roses . . . He saw a rose in particular, a white one. . .

## IV

The day passed in elegant conversation, as is the way with the landed gentry all the world over. Lord Paramour and Miss Lyon-West, beautiful in vermilion *organdie*, went for a walk in the afternoon; but on their return Mrs. Lyon-West observed on her daughter's cheeks none of those signs of pretty confusion which denote a happy consummation; they were still the pale cheeks of a young lady of fashion; they were unmantled.

Now it has frequently been said of Mrs. Lyon-West that she is indiscreet; but never that she is not brave.

That night, when the gentlemen had joined the ladies, and Mrs. Custard had retired, saying she had to go to Paris early in the morning as she was very short of long gloves, Mrs. Lyon-West addressed herself to Lord Paramour brightly:

"I hope," she said, "that you enjoyed your walk in the rose garden?"

"Enchanting!" said Lord Paramour. "Enchanting."

"I'm *so* glad you liked it," breathed Mrs. Lyon-West; and she looked at him steadfastly, the brave woman. "Well, Lord Paramour?"

"Ah," said Lord Paramour thoughtfully.

She created a diversion by requiring a light for her cigarette, which Mr. Soda, with his well-known *galanterie*, instantly supplied.

"The only thing I'm not sure about," whispered Lord Paramour, "is whether I like her nose. Sorry, I'm sure."

# The Loquacious Lady of
# Lansdowne Passage

This is a story about my friend George Tarlyon, who is a brave man and no bigger liar than most. Of course, George Tarlyon ought to know better than to be afraid of walking through Lansdowne Passage at night. But you can tell him that until you are blue in the face and he will smile at you and agree with you, but still he will not walk through Lansdowne Passage at night, saying that he is afraid. And when you ask him of what he is afraid, he will smile a shameless smile and reply that he gives Lansdowne Passage a miss because he is afraid of meeting a woman in it. At that you will at once express impatience, disbelief, and disgust, for on no female occasion whatsoever will you have noticed upon George Tarlyon's brow that cold sweat which denotes a decent bashfulness in a man. And then, maybe, you will jeer at George Tarlyon, forgetting for a moment that he is a head taller than any quick-tempered man should be, and thinking to goad him into revelation of the reason or reasons why he, a noted warrior on many fields from Ranelagh to Vimy Ridge, should be afraid of meeting a woman in Lansdowne Passage. And maybe George Tarlyon will tell you, and maybe he will not.

In these days of easy travelling and tourist facilities it need scarcely be explained that Lansdowne Passage is a narrow path between two high walls; and that this path is carved between the princely domains of Devonshire House and Lansdowne House. Men speak of a time when, midway through the passage, they had every now and then to pass under a light wooden bridge which had overnight been thrown from the top of one high wall to the other, and how it seemed to them pleasant to think that perhaps the Marquess of Lansdowne was going to step across to visit the Duke of Devonshire that day. But nothing like that happens nowadays, for Devonshire House emptily awaits its destiny and Lansdowne House is held in fief by a distinguished stranger. But there is still something feudal about Lansdowne Passage, for it is a private right-of-way, and on one day every year Lord Lansdowne sends his men to lock and bolt the doors at each end of the passage, as it is his right to do, for the only way a man has of showing that a passage is his passage is by keeping every one else out of it for one day every year, the date to be left to his discretion. Through Lansdowne Passage, on 364 days of the year, the pedestrian (or two pedestrians abreast, but not more than two, for you can't have everything) can walk direct from Curzon Street to Berkeley Street, and thus save himself an endless amount of walking round by Piccadilly or Berkeley Square. Mention must also be made of an old man who, on 364 days of the year, wanders about the passage with a broom, or sometimes leans the broom against the wall and sits down on the upturned end of a narrow wooden box, which he brings with him every morning for that purpose; but he doesn't really have very much time for sitting on his box, for all autumn he sweeps away at the leaves, happily without effect, and for the rest of the year you cannot drop a piece of paper, orange-peel, or cigarette-end without having it swept away at once; and all the year round he gives you greeting as you pass, in a friendly way.

Now, one night in May, a year after the world was said to be at peace, George Tarlyon had reason to be walking in a westerly direction from Dover Street; down Hay Hill he went, and down the covered stairway from Berkeley Street into Lansdowne Passage. The hour was very late, the night pleasantly dark and cool, and the stillness of a sleeping city broken only by the cameo noises of the narrow hours. His steps rang gaily between the high walls of the passage, echoes carelessly tossing themselves from one wall to the other, round and about and every way, and he was almost half-way through before he realised that he was sharing the passage with another: a woman just ahead of him, walking slowly in his direction, but scarcely walking, loitering against the wall, a self-effacing woman of the night. George Tarlyon passed her, and about her face he was not at all curious. A word followed him, a shy word, but he strode on, two steps, three steps—and then another word followed him, louder, and he swung round, not very amiably.

Now the words which women of the night cast into the night as a lure for passing men are few, and their expression limited; and many had been cast to George Tarlyon in passing but never had he chosen one, for that kind of thing did not amuse him, and he was quite popular enough in his own circle. But "My dear!" this woman had cried at his back, softly, not at all insinuatingly: a ladylike voice, without glitter or suggestion, just appealing; and it somehow caught the drum of George Tarlyon's ear, the gentle "my dear," and he swung round to it.

"Well?" asked George Tarlyon, not very amiably. But he made a gesture towards his hat, which is more than most men do on the casual occasion.

She softly came towards him, and stood a long way below him, for she was a short, slight woman: of about middle years, and of the middle sort, plain featured and dressed unnoticeably: very quiet and ladylike she was. From one hand hung a bag, just a little larger than those called hand-bags, and full-looking, as might be that of a sempstress or governess who is absent from her home all day. The little lady smiled, without lure. . . .

"Well?" asked George Tarlyon again, not very amiably.

"It's only," said the little lady, "that I am afraid to walk alone through this passage, and would be very grateful if you would

allow me to walk with you as far as the Curzon Street end."
Very quiet and ladylike she was.

"Why, of course," said George Tarlyon, politely enough, and
more or less dismissed the thing with a swing round. But the
little lady walked as slowly with him as she had without him,
and he had to accommodate his step to hers.

"But if you're afraid," George Tarlyon just thought to ask,
"aren't you even more afraid of addressing a stranger, who
might do a little lady some harm in a lonely place like this?"

The little lady smiled gently.

"I saw your face as you passed," she said. "You might be
dangerous to a lady in a drawing-room but not in Lansdowne
Passage. Unlike some men I know. . . ."

They were walking very slowly, and still had almost half of the
passage to go, but George Tarlyon did not say "Hurry up, little
lady," thinking she was a pathetic little thing, more than usually
pathetic of her kind. But he was not interested in her, and it was
only out of politeness that he asked:

"Have you had trouble with one or two, then?"

"With one," she told him softly. She was so small, and he so
tall, that her voice seemed to float up to him from somewhere
about his knees. He scarcely listened to it. To tell the truth, he
was rather tired. "With one," she repeated. "That is why I am
afraid of walking through here by myself at night. It happened
many years ago, but every detail is still very clear to me."

"He must have frightened you a good deal," said George
Tarlyon. Not that he was interested.

"I wouldn't say that," said the little lady gently. "But it was
certainly the most important thing that has ever happened in
my life. You see, sir, I had to get three pounds that night. I had
already made two pounds, for that is all I have ever dared to ask,
though sometimes the kinder gentlemen have given me more,
but that night I had to make three pounds more, for five
pounds a week was the rent of my rooms and already overdue

sometime. . . ." The gentle voice ran on, floating up to him from somewhere about his knee, and he scarcely listened. They were quite near the Curzon Street end now, and the words floated upwards quicker. . . .

"Just about where you passed me, I spoke to him—in the passage here. He was a short man, and not a gentleman, but I needed three pounds badly and nowadays you never know who has money and who hasn't, do you? But as soon as he answered and looked at me I knew I had made a mistake, but there's no use being rude, and so I walked on with him. He said something about the coolness of the weather, but although I kept my eyes in front of me, not liking the look of him, you see, I knew very well that he was taking me in sideways. There's no use being silly, I told myself, but I did wish I hadn't got my two pounds in my bag or that someone else would come into the passage, though there's generally little chance of that at this hour of night, unless it's a policeman to smoke a cigarette. And so I hurried on as quick as I could to get to Curzon Street, and we weren't more than half-way through this passage then, but he got hold of my arm and stopped me quick enough. I didn't look at his eyes, for I'd seen them once, you see, but I heard him asking for money, as I knew he would. And then he got hold of my bag by the strap, but I held on tight, saying there was naught in it but powder and a handkerchief, but still not looking at his eyes for I knew their kind well enough. But he held on, and said he would give me some cocaine, 'snow' he called it, if I let him have money, and with his other hand he fumbled in his pocket. 'I'll scream,' I said, and at that he let go of my bag quick enough, so I could hurry on to Curzon Street. He dropped back then, but I was in such a state to get to Curzon Street that I couldn't hear him behind me for the beating of my heart. But behind me he must have been, for I'd just got to within a yard—why, we're at the spot now, I *have* been slow in telling!—when from behind his hand clapped me over the mouth, and I heard his breathing very hoarse at my neck, and then a sharp funny pain in the shoulder-blade took me. As sharp as a knife, they say, but this was a knife, and ever so sharp in the shoulder-blade it was—but it didn't hurt so much as feel funny, if you understand, and everything was so mixed up—his breathing, and the funny feeling in the shoulder-blade, and somewhere a clock striking once, but I went off before it struck again, for it must have been on three o'clock. I never thought death would be like that."

And George Tarlyon looked for the little lady and he saw only the wall, and George Tarlyon ran headlong out of Lansdowne Passage, and as he ran he heard a clock strike the last two notes of three o'clock.

# The Smell in the Library

## I

One night we were at a party, George Tarlyon and I, and there were also present some other people. It was not, however, a good party, and we left it before eleven o'clock. I cannot remember now how it was that one had gone there so early, but anyway it is of no significance. As we passed out, a misguided fellow said it would get better later on, but I extracted him from Tarlyon's teeth, and so out into the street. A long string of cars stretched from the door towards Park Lane, and here and there chauffeurs stood in sombre groups, and we wondered if they thought they were missing anything. The heat of the crowded rooms had put us in a fever, the night air penetrated our flimsy evening-coats, and we shivered and murmured. From the open windows of the house we had left there followed us down the length of Green Street that asinine blare which is the punishment of England for having lost America; and George Tarlyon muttered that there ought to be a law to prevent people from giving fat-headed parties full of crashing bores and plain women, the joints of whose knees cracked in trying any dance which their mothers had not danced before them. I tried to soothe him and myself by saying that parties were not what they were and there it was; but he would not be soothed, for he had been given a glass of cider-cup in mistake for champagne, and he who touches cider-cup in the watches of the night may neither forget nor forgive.

We walked up Park Lane aimlessly, for we knew not what to do nor whither to go. We were further elated by the fact that we could sum up only one cigarette between us.

I suggested that one might do worse than go to bed, but Tarlyon said it was too early for that. "It is never too early," I said morosely, "to go to bed."

"Pah!" said Tarlyon, and so we walked down Park Lane.

Now it is frequently said that Park Lane is full of Jews, but very few met our eyes, and they might quite well have been Gentiles. There are many illusions prevalent in the provinces about life in the great metropolis of London: such as *(a)* that it is gay: *(b)* that it is wicked: *(c)* that boys will be boys: *(d)* that there is plenty to do when it rains: *(e)* that you have only to go for a walk to see many "well-dressed women in costly furs"; but the one which has even less foundation in fact than any of these is that, life in a great city being what it is, there is never an hour of the twenty-four when the great streets are not, to a student of life, full of matter for observation. But, as George Tarlyon said, you might be a student of life until you burst and still find no matter for observation—though here we were in Park Lane and the hour not yet eleven!

"The whole thing is a ramp," we said. "Now take this matter about the Jews. We have been distinctly given to understand that this Lane is full of Jews—but what do we see? Two 'buses and a policeman. But that leads us to an interesting speculation: can a policeman be a Jew? Has such a thing as a Jewish policeman ever been seen or heard of? And if not, what is it that prevents a policeman from being a Jew? Is the religious feeling among policemen stronger than that among Privy Councillors?"

"Let's ask him," I suggested. The policeman was decorating the corner of Upper Brook Street. Tarlyon asked him, and the policeman said that Vine Street was not so far off as all that, while as for Marlborough Street, it was even nearer. He wasn't there to be accosted, he wasn't, said the policeman wickedly.

"Ho!" said Tarlyon. "And have you been arresting any more respectable old clergymen in Hyde Park for talking to women without an introduction from a bishop? Blast me but I wouldn't dream of entering Hyde Park nowadays, not at night anyway, without a battalion of chaps fringed with torpedo-netting."

"Good-night, constable," I said hurriedly.

"Good-night, sir," said he—a discreet man.

"Pah!" said Tarlyon.

We walked up Park Lane.

And suddenly Tarlyon gripped my arm, and waved his stick and whispered—

"Look at that! Ralph, just look at that!"

Ten yards or so ahead of us loomed the back of a giant. He was striding on with huge steps, a black cloak was flung about him, and he wore no hat. Maybe it was the cloak, swaying this way and that, and one end flapping over a shoulder, that made the man seem taller than he really was—but it was a colossal back.

"It's reminiscent," Tarlyon murmured. "I can't help a feeling about that back—it's reminiscent."

"It's reminiscent," I whispered, "of a back I once lent money to. One hundred pounds it was. . . ."

We quickened our pace. The huge figure passed under the light of a lamp, and the light fell on his bare head, and his hair flamed up like fire.

The huge figure, the arrogant walk, the flaming ginger hair. . . .

"Red Antony!" I murmured.

"And we thought he was dead!" muttered Tarlyon—as though Red Antony could have died without the noise of his death-rattle confounding the thunder of the guns that killed many better men! Could a man who lived so noisily die as other men? And yet, because the lean years of peace had passed without sight or sign of him, we had believed the rumour that had had it that Sir Antony Poole had risen to be sergeant in a Canadian storm battalion and had then died; which had seemed natural in a kind of way, for the worst German shot couldn't, one thought, have consistently missed six-foot-four under a crown of flaming hair.

If there was a man who did not know, or know of, Antony Poole in the careless years before the war, then there must have been something the matter with his eyes or ears. For Red Antony was a famous sight in every crowded place in London, and achieved considerable nonentity as the noisiest and worst-tempered rascal since Fighting Fitzgerald of the Regency. He crashed, did Antony, in furious idiocy from row to row and roguery to roguery, so that the day inevitably came when no decent man or woman would be seen speaking to the man. Oh, a calamitous pair, the brothers Poole! For one night his brother, the great Sir Roger, brilliant and sardonic Roger, dark and successful Roger, good sportsman and lovable fellow—one night our Roger put a bullet through his head, and at the inquest the amazed world heard that he had done this unbelievable thing because the police were hammering at the door with a warrant for his arrest on a charge of fraud. This we, his friends, did not believe. The police may have been hammering at the door, we said, but the police are notoriously promiscuous about the doors they hammer at. "Fraud be damned in connection with Roger Poole!"—that is what we said. Why, he was fine, that Roger—*fine*! Thus we mourned him, once the wealthiest and wittiest of our company, and we defended his memory against the few who dared impugn it. But the disappearance of the red giant who was now Sir Antony Poole we did not mourn, for from the day of the inquest, at which he broke down and wept like a stricken child, he had not been seen in London until this night in Park Lane.

## II

"Go quietly," Tarlyon restrained me. "We'll learn Red Antony to walk up Park Lane without a hat."

Gently we approached, one on each side of the colossal back. "Oi!" we cried.

A wrench, and he faced us. We are tall, but we were as children beneath him.

"Oi to you!" snarled Antony. "Who the blazes are you, anyway?" And the great red expanse which was given to Antony for a face surveyed us intolerantly. Never what you might call an easy-tempered man, Red Antony.

"We be friends," said Tarlyon sombrely.

"That's uncommonly original of you," drawled Antony. "I didn't know I had any." And he pretended not to recognise us—for Antony must always act, always play cussed.

"You haven't," Tarlyon grinned. "But mine was just a manner of speaking." He knew his man; and there passed over Red Antony's face that earthquake and tornado which was given him for a smile and a laugh.

"Hell! Always the same Tarlyon! How are you, George?"

"Monstrous," says George.

"But there is no sensation in matter," boomed Red Antony, crushing his hand.

"And this," said Tarlyon, waving his other towards me, "and this, Sir Antony, is your old friend Ralph Wyndham Trevor, whom you may quite well have forgotten, since you owe him a hundred pounds."

Another earthquake across that vast red expanse, so that I feared for the sleep of those mythical Jews. . . .

"Dear old Trevor—fancy having kept you waiting all this time! Here you are, man, here you are." And from somewhere inside his cloak he jerked a pocket-book into my hand and crushed it against my palm. "You can keep the change, old boy, as you're younger than I am and look as though you need it. Always take vegetables with your meat, Trevor."

"I hate to take money from an impoverished baronet," I got in, just to goad him.

"Impoverished nothing!" he boomed, and swung on Tarlyon, who backed a step. "D'you remember, George, that Roger always said I had a *flair* for making money—"

"But he added," Tarlyon said, "that you hadn't got the brain of a louse to back that *flair* up with."

Boomed Antony: "I have studied the ways of lice for five years on end and must inform you, George, that my brain, though moth-eaten, is certainly superior. I have made mints of money. I am fat with money. I roll in money. . . ." He was working himself up into that state of chronic excitement in which he might twist the lamp-post. Breakable or twistable things had always a fascination for Red Antony.

"There, there!" I soothed him. "And we thought the little man was dead!"

"There, there!" said George. "Did he make money, now! And we thought he was lying in some forgotten foreign field with a German bullet in his heart."

Bother the man! He simply had to make a noise each time he opened his mouth. The policeman who had talked Vine Street to us approached.

"Dead! Me dead!" And the sweep of his arm flung wide his cloak, and indeed he looked a mighty man of wrath. "As though a Prooshian bullet could kill me!"

"You are no doubt reserved for a more terrible end," said Tarlyon.

Blessed if the man didn't wilt! That roaring red giant—he wilted.

"Don't say that, George," he begged hoarsely. "It's a fool remark to make, that. You didn't mean it, did you?" And he put the question seriously! We gaped at him.

"He was only being funny," I explained. "He tries his best. . . ."

"I wish you well, Antony," said Tarlyon, out of his surprise.

"God, I need it!" Antony growled surprisingly.

And then I laughed—remembering Red Antony's old way of acting cussed, just to surprise and annoy. He'd do anything to make a fool of someone, that man, even if he had to make a fool of himself in doing it. But as I laughed, Antony looked at me with furious, haggard eyes, and I stopped laughing.

I saw Tarlyon looking at him queerly. He knew Antony much better than I did, for many and many a year ago he was a junior subaltern in the mess when Antony threw a bottle at the head of an extremely superior officer. The bottle was full, the aim was true, and Antony was cashiered with all due pomp and dishonour. But, through all his subsequent follies, Tarlyon had liked him. One couldn't, of course, defend Antony; but the very few who had once liked Red Antony always, somehow, went on liking him. There was something about the man, a sort of tremendous gallantry, an air of shameless bravado, a thunder of individuality, which might have made him a simple and lovable giant—but for a grain of rotten subtlety somewhere in him. Fine timber worm-eaten, Tarlyon said. Not, of course, said Tarlyon, that himself was anything to write home about.

"What's the matter, old Antony?" Tarlyon asked kindly. "You've changed enormously. . . ."

Now I had noticed no particular change, except, perhaps, that handsome Antony looked his forty years and more; but Tarlyon knew him better.

"How have I changed?" snapped Antony. He hated kindness; he thought he was being pitied.

"You look a bit worn, old boy, that's all," said George lightly.

"If it comes to that, you aren't the man you were, what with war, wine, and women!"

"Talking of wine," I thought to say, "one always understood that you'd die of drink, Antony. That's probably what George meant when he said you looked worn."

I wished I had kept my mouth shut. His eyes blazed over me. . . . but he restrained himself; and Antony's "restraint" was a portentous business—it made a noise like a fast car with the brakes jammed on.

"Drink!" he said sharply. "I drink nothing to speak of nowadays. There's an end to all things. . . ." Now the lion's bedside manner is a significant thing, and even more significant is it when the lion in the fullness of his strength sways a little, just a little; and what would make Red Antony sway just a little would be enough to put another man under the table, and no dishonour to the strength of his head, either.

"I do not wish," said Antony reasonably, "that you should think me irresponsible through excess of stimulant. The things that are happening to me are not happening through drink, and you must bear that in mind. I am saner than a sane man, though I can hear and see and smell things that a sane man would die of. . . ."

Tarlyon looked at me meaningly. Antony seemed to have forgotten us. Tarlyon took his arm.

"We can't stay here all night," he said. "Let us now leave Park Lane in a body and go to my house. . . ."

Antony woke up; he threw back his head and howled: "Taxi!"

"All right, sir, all right," said the policeman gently. "You don't need to shout like that." That was a brave policeman.

"I insist on shouting," boomed Antony. "Taxi!"

And, thankfully, a taxi appeared from Mount Street, for Red Antony and the police never did mix well. He once arrested two policemen for loitering and took them to Vine Street. . . .

Antony flung open the door. A clock began the lengthy job of striking eleven o'clock.

"We will go to *my* house," said Antony. "I have a charming house, and an appointment to keep in it. Jump in." We jumped in, and we heard him give the driver the address of a house in Regent's Park. How often had we not directed taxis to that house! Tarlyon whistled.

"So you've got Roger's old house!" he murmured.

Antony did not answer. The taxi staggered northwards as best it could.

"I don't see," snapped Antony at last, "why you should gape about it. Getting back to England four months ago, I found the house empty, and took it. It seems natural enough."

"I never said it wasn't," Tarlyon murmured. But he thought it wasn't, and so did I. A brother, on coming back to civilisation after many years' absence, does not immediately leap into the house in which his elder brother blew his brains out—anyway, I wouldn't.

The taxi twisted through the gates, round the little drive, and to the great door. An odd feeling it was, to stand again in front of that door after nine years—but now we faced a house black and still where once had been a house of shining windows, gay with music and the laughter of the most brilliant company in London. Oh, the Georgians, the magnificent young Georgians—mostly dead!

We told the driver to wait, and followed Antony in. We stood still in the pitch-black hall until he should switch on the light, and in the blaze of light in which the cloaked figure faced us I instantly understood what Tarlyon had meant when he said that Antony had "changed." I can only describe the change by saying that the structure of his face seemed to have fallen into disrepair; its brick-red complexion of old had dwindled to a faint pink, so that one had an idea that any ordinary face would have been a ghastly white; and he looked worn with more than the usual wear of passing years. But the wild eyes were still wild, and uncommonly fine he looked as he faced us in the sombre hall, the huge dandy in the black cloak with the head of flaming hair brushed immaculately back.

He smiled at us with that sudden charm for which women had forgiven him much—too much; he flung out an arm in the grand manner.

"Welcome to the old house," he said. "And for heaven's sake try to look as though you didn't miss Roger."

But the magic of Roger Poole was not, I thought, in the place; the house was now but a shell for a noisy man.

### III

"Champagne is indicated," said Antony; and that indication led us to the dining-room—a long, oak-panelled room at the back of the house. The curtains were not drawn across the two French windows, which gave out to a lawn sloping carelessly down to the water of Regent's Park; and in the second in which Antony fumbled for the electric switch the dark shapes of the trees looked like the van of an impenetrable forest. But dark shapes of trees always look more or less like that.

"Didn't you say something about an appointment?" Tarlyon asked vaguely, as Antony ravished the wire off a bottle.

"Did I?" He looked up at us from his business, very thoughtfully. "Oh, did I?"

"Pop!" said the champagne cork.

We drank, and Antony looked at his wrist-watch.

"Damn!" he said. "It's stopped."

"The time being just 11.25," I helped him.

"Thanks," said Antony, very mild, very thoughtful. "Excuse me a moment, will you?" And he strode across the room to the folding doors which led to Roger's old library and card-room. He closed the door behind him, but it did not catch, swung open a few inches. No light filled the dark vertical space.

"Never known him so polite before," I muttered.

"He's absent-minded," said Tarlyon, looking thoughtfully at the dark space.

"What I want to know," he whispered, "is what he's doing in there in the dark?"

"Keeping his appointment," I suggested facetiously.

Tarlyon looked from the door to me.

"Poor devil!" he said softly. I thought he was pitying me for my wit, of which I was never very proud.

He put down his empty glass, dug his hands into his pockets, and lounged to the folding-doors. I never knew a man who could walk so casually as Tarlyon; you never expected him to get anywhere, but he always got there before you expected him to.

He kicked the slightly open door a little wider with the tip of his shoe. I was just behind his shoulder.

"Antony!" he called softly.

From the light in which we stood the library was a pit of darkness. Nothing moved in the pit. There was no sound.

"He's not there," I whispered; and I wondered why I whispered.

"Can you smell anything?" a hoarse voice suddenly asked from the darkness.

Tarlyon lounged into the black room. But, somehow, I did not feel called upon to follow. I leant against the door.

Deeply set in the darkness I could at last make out the faintly white patch which must be Antony's shirt-front; and I wondered what tomfoolery he was up to now, asking stupid questions in a startling voice out of a poisonously dark room. I could smell nothing at all, and didn't expect to.

"What kind of a smell?" Tarlyon asked—in a reasonable tone! He stood just within the door, his back to me.

"Can you smell *nothing* at all?" the hoarse, subdued voice asked again. "But, of course, it's very faint now."

Tarlyon put up his nose and sniffed. I sniffed. More than faint it was, I thought.

"Been smoking?" Tarlyon asked, and he sniffed again.

"No," came a whisper.

"Oh," said Tarlyon. This was lunatic talk, and I was just about to say so when Antony asked sharply:

"Why did you ask?"

"I thought I smelt smoke," said Tarlyon. "Might be cigarette smoke."

"It is," I snapped, for I was smoking a Turkish cigarette just behind his ear.

"You blasted fool!" said Antony—and with such contempt behind it that from being bored I got annoyed. I stretched out my hand on the inside of the library door and switched on the light.

"Turn that out, you fool!" came a frantic roar, and I had a vision of a red giant murdering the distance between us. I've never thanked God for anything so much as for having directed the body of George Tarlyon to be standing between Red Antony and myself. I turned off the light quick enough.

"Steady, Antony, steady!" said Tarlyon.

"Oh, go to hell!" growled Antony.

I thought to myself that we couldn't be very far from it at the moment. But the spell, or smell, it seemed, was broken. I was thankful for that, anyway.

Back in the lighted dining-room Antony emptied his glass; and grinned at me rather shamefacedly.

"Sorry, old boy," he said. I grinned back, as though I had enjoyed it.

Tarlyon asked suddenly:

"Have you got a spare bedroom for me, Antony?"

I stared, Antony stared. Then Antony smiled, and never before had I seen him smile quite like that.

"Thank you, George," he said, almost softly. "Now that's really a friendly action. But I'll be all right—you needn't worry."

Then he addressed me as well; I had never seen Antony so reasonable.

"Come to dinner here to-morrow night," he begged. "Both of you. I can give you quite a good dinner." He seemed very earnest, looking from one to the other of us. I was going to say I was engaged, but Tarlyon answered quickly:

"Right, Antony." And because he looked at me in a certain way, I let it be.

## IV

In the taxi, at last, Tarlyon said:

"Ralph, you risked your life by turning on that light, but you did a great service."

"What do you mean?"

"Didn't you see anything?"

I then lost my temper.

"No," I shouted. "I neither smelt anything in the dark nor saw anything in the light, except that red lunatic charging at me."

"He was only preserving his illusion," Tarlyon said mildly. "Didn't you see, in that second of light, the open desk just by us, beside the door?"

"I saw nothing but Antony, but quite enough of him."

"Pity. If you had seen the desk, you would have seen a telephone overturned on it, the receiver hanging down, and a revolver on the floor."

This was getting serious. I struck a match and examined Tarlyon's face. He was not smiling.

"Fact," he assured me. "You would have seen the desk just as it was after Roger Poole had shot himself at it."

"You don't mean—"

"I mean, old boy, that Antony has gone and put everything back exactly as he last saw it in Roger's library. Roger, Roger's wife, Antony and another fellow were in the dining-room. The telephone-bell rang in the library and Roger went to answer it, telling Antony to come with him. He didn't turn on the light in the library. The telephone told Roger that the police were after him. And the two in the dining-room heard Roger telling Antony what he thought of him as a man and brother, then they heard a shot; and when they got to the door and switched on the light, they saw Roger dead at the desk and Antony standing where he was standing to-night. Antony went out by the window into the garden—and he has reconstructed the scene exactly as he last saw it, even to a dummy telephone and a revolver! In fact, everything is there except Roger. Silly, isn't it?"

Silly was not the word. "But why, why?"

"That's what I want to find out," said Tarlyon. "Antony is playing some sort of a game with himself, and he's frightening himself to death in doing it. He always was a superstitious ass. Giants usually are, somehow—perhaps because, having nothing physical to fear, they fear the psychic. I'll bet he goes into that library every night at the same time—Roger shot himself at about twenty-five past eleven, by the way. Poor old Antony!"

"But what was all that nonsense about the smell?" I asked.

Tarlyon did not answer. At last he said:

"Did you ever hear, Ralph, the theory that if Judas Iscariot had not come after Jesus he might have done all that Jesus did? But as he found he could not because he was too late, he was doomed to crime. In a sort of far-fetched way it was the same with Roger and Antony. The tragedy of those two brothers has something absurdly, fantastically reasonable about it. You see, Roger was a year older and did all that Antony wanted to do, the fine and brilliant things, while poor Antony could do nothing but make a fool of himself, which he did only too well. Antony would have been a man of many accomplishments, for he's no fool, but for the fact that Roger was before him—so Antony thought. And Roger loved Antony, while Antony hated and admired and feared Roger. And at last, somehow or another, he managed to betray Roger. No one knows what that last moment held for those two—no one knows what lay behind the insults that Roger heaped on Antony at that final moment. For they were overheard, you know, by Roger's wife and the man who was dining there. But something seems to have stuck in Antony's mind and grown very big with years. I'm rather concerned for the poor devil, Ralph. He's still afraid of his elder brother. Or perhaps he feels that Roger left something unsaid which he must hear, and so he wants to recreate him."

It was as the taxi stopped at my door that Tarlyon cried out as though he had made a discovery:

"Good God, of course!"

"Of course what?"

"Smoke, you fool! It *was* smoke!"

## V

What was our surprise, on entering the dining-room some minutes after nine o'clock the next evening—for Antony dined late—to see the table laid for four! And then a lady came in—a tall, dark young lady, a strange and unusual lady with a flash of very white teeth for a smile and a gardenia alight on the wing of her sleek black hair! I am afraid Tarlyon and I must have seemed very rude, for we were so surprised that we stared. The white teeth flashed at us. We bowed.

"My wife," said Antony. We bowed again. She was the sort of woman one bowed to. Antony's wife!

"Diavalen," said Antony abruptly, "this is Lord Tarlyon and Mr. Trevor."

Diavalen—Lady Poole!—said nothing. With that wonderful trick of flashing those wonderful teeth she didn't need to say anything.

"She's a Creole," said Antony, as we sat at the table. He said it as he might have said that she was an orange. Those white teeth flashed at me, and I smiled back, feeling an ass. There didn't seem much to say about her being a Creole. . . .

I don't know how Tarlyon felt about it, but it took me some time to get my wind. "My wife," says Antony! Never a word nor a sign about being married—to that glorious, dark, alien creature with the flashing teeth and sleek black hair! Diavalen the Creole! Just like Red Antony to marry a Creole called

Diavalen and then spring her on to you with a "my wife."
I remembered Antony once saying, years and years ago: "Never
give away gratuitous information, old boy." But there are limits.
And one of them is to have a wife with flashing teeth, a gardenia
in her hair, and a name like Diavalen, and then throw her in
with the soup.

Red Antony was never what you might call a good host: not,
particularly, at the beginning of dinner. To-night he was
morose. But Tarlyon talked—to Lady Poole. It would take more
than a lovely Creole to baffle Tarlyon. He seemed to have inside
information as to what were the subjects best calculated to
excite interest in a Creole married to a morose English baronet
with ginger hair. Diavalen did not talk. But one did not realise
that she wasn't talking, for she was wonderfully expressive with
her smiling, flashing, teeth. She seemed to have discovered the
art of using teeth for something besides eating.

As Tarlyon talked to her she turned her face towards him, and
of this I took advantage to stare at her face bit by bit. The
perfection of that face was a challenge to a right-thinking man.
"It is too small," I thought. But it was not too small. "It is too
white," I thought. But it was not too white. For quite a long time
I could not wrench my eyes away from those flashing teeth and
scarlet curling lips—they fascinated me. Her face was white, the
gardenia in her hair looked almost yellow beside the whiteness
of Diavalen's face; and I thought to myself that that white
complexion was a considerable achievement, for I was sure her
skin underneath was faintly, deliciously brown. It was a small
face. It was a decoration, enchanting and unreal. And in the
decoration were painted in luminous paint two large black eyes;
the eyelashes swept over them, often she half closed them—
they were very lazy black eyes; and deep in them there was a
sheen, as of a reflection of distant fire. I did not like the lady's
eyes very much, I don't know why. But as to that sleek black hair
in which lay a gardenia like a light in silken darkness—you felt

that you simply must run your hand over that hair to see if it was as beautifully sleek and silky as it looked, and you wouldn't have minded betting that it was. She was the most strangely lovely woman I have ever seen. And she was the most silent.

Even Tarlyon was at last baffled by the silence of Diavalen. A silence fell. The teeth flashed at me, and I was just about to say something to her when Antony's voice hit the drum of my ear and I dropped my fork.

"I shouldn't trouble," said Antony. "She's dumb."

That is why I dropped my fork. The servant picked it up and gave me another. I made a considerable business of it, and then I ate furiously. Red Antony, vile Antony! I didn't look at Tarlyon. He was furious, I knew. He was a man who did not take a very liberal view of jokes like that. But the worst of Antony was that he didn't care what view any one took; he just said the first thing that came into his great red head.

If the dinner (which was excellent as to food and wine) had been a frost before, it was, naturally, not a howling success after that. The only thing to do was to pretend that Antony had not spoken. It seemed too silly to say to the lovely Creole: "Oh, I'm *so* sorry!" Poor Diavalen! But I couldn't pretend, I simply could not find anything to say which didn't need an answer. Just try being suddenly planted with a dumb woman and see if conversation flows naturally from you.

Tarlyon and Antony talked about English heavyweight boxers. Antony was himself a super-heavyweight, and seemed to have a poor opinion of English heavyweights. He wanted to know whether their weight was calculated by the noise they made on being smitten to the ground in the first round. He said that he was tired of opening a newspaper only to read of the domestic history of Famous British Boxers and of seeing photographs of the wives, mothers and children of Famous British Boxers. He said that the whole idea of the press was to impress on the public how gentle, amiable and loving Famous British Boxers were in the home. He pointed out that the whole trouble lay in the fact that Famous British Boxers were too damned gentle, amiable, and loving in the ring. In fact, Antony, having put the lid on his wife, had woken up.

Then, at last, Diavalen rose, and we rose. I rushed to the door and held it open. Her teeth flashed at Tarlyon, and he bowed like a courtier. As she passed Antony, he said, "Good-night, Diavalen," but he said it as though he didn't care whether her night was good or bad. As she passed Antony she gave him a look out of her large, black eyes. I was glad I did not know what that look said, but I was sure that Antony deserved it. "Good-night, Lady Poole," I said; teeth flashed at me, a touch of pleasant scent hovered faintly, and Diavalen was gone.

"Heavens, she's lovely!" I whispered, as I joined them at the table.

Tarlyon's fingers played with the stem of his port-glass.

"Would you mind explaining, Antony," he asked dangerously, "why you chose that infamous way of telling us that your wife was—well, not quite like the rest of us?" There was, I agreed, something blasphemous about the ghastly word "dumb" in relation to that lovely creature.

Red Antony leant back in his chair and dug his hands deep in his pockets, so that his white shirt-front stuck out like the breast-plate of a warrior. He looked bored.

"Favourite trick of hers," he explained morosely. "Always tries to act as though she wasn't dumb. If you had to live with that silly pretence it would get on your nerves, I can tell you. She does it very well, I admit. Takes a pride in it—making a fool of other people, I call it. On board ship from New York she put it over quite a number of people for a day or two. Lord, it would have got on anyone's nerves, the way she grinned and grinned and showed her teeth! Why not be honest and say one's dumb and be done with it? Or let me say it! There's no crime in being dumb, especially with a beautiful face like that. But she won't see it, she must smile and flash her teeth—she's got a repertoire of grins that would astonish a movie star; and she's so proud of them that even if she could speak she wouldn't. And sometimes all that grinning and toothwork gets me so raw that I could put back my head and howl—and she knows it. Sorry I offended you, George. But I'm nervy these days. I'm raw—*raw*!" He shouted that last word at us with a thump on the table; and raw he looked, with the eyes blazing out of him, and his once huge, once red, once jolly face shrunk to a mockery of itself, with the skin drawn tight across his jaws and hollow in the cheeks.

Tarlyon picked up a liqueur-glass which the thump had upset. "Sorry about your unhappy marriage, Antony," he said, "But, you know, it takes a Napoleon to marry a beautiful Creole. How did it happen?"

"How?" And Antony laughed; at least he made a noise which was perhaps intended to sound like laughter. "How? Because she made it happen—how else? D'you think because she's dumb that she hasn't got more fascination than a thousand women rolled together? Those eyes? Met eyes like that before, George? If hell has a face its eyes will be like that. I *had* to marry her . . . In Mexico where I went to after the Armistice. I suppose you fellows remember that I went to Mexico three years before the war. I was in love with the girl who became Roger's wife—inevitable, wasn't it, that the only woman I ever loved should fall to Roger? He didn't do it on purpose, of course—it just happened. So I went to Mexico, to try to do something which Roger could not do before me. Last chance kind of thing, you know—" The rain of words faded out of him. He had moved considerably from the subject of Diavalen, but who could hold a haunted face like that to a subject? I wished I could, for I didn't want him to run amok about Roger. There was something—well, indecent, in talking about a man dead nine years or more as though he were alive and still wanting to "put it across" Antony at every turn. I wished Tarlyon would say something, but he was silent, his fingers fiddling with the stem of his port-glass. Antony was drinking next to nothing; round about his coffee-cup were at least six quarter-smoked cigarettes, and now he began to maul a cigar. I never saw him smoke that cigar.

"In Mexico," Antony said softly, "I found oil. It was very good oil, as Roger said later, but there wasn't much of it. My luck again! But I made Roger share it this time. You remember how I reappeared in England? Through that window over there, while Roger was giving a big dinner-party, sitting where I'm sitting now. You were here, George. Roger and I made it up before the lot of you—after a silence of years. Entirely on my side, the quarrel—Roger always loved me. We made it up, you remember, George? I wanted, you see, to plant Roger with that oil. Cascan Oil—it sounded like a big thing at the time. That was the last big dinner-party Roger ever gave. He was unhappy at home—some love misunderstanding—and he took to me, Roger did. He went head over heels into that bucket-shop. Of course he soon saw through me and my oil—the man wasn't born who could take Roger in—but he let the company go on. He wanted to see how far I'd go. Giving me my head, you know. He had packets of money in reserve, and thought he could put the thing right any moment. But he got reckless—watching me and wondering how far I'd go. Roger had always loved me ever since we were children—he never thought of me but as a naughty baby with a bee in my red head about him. I could see all the time he was wondering how far I *dared* go. And he was unhappy at home, poor Roger; he and his wife somehow couldn't get their particular ways of loving each other to work well together. So he had nothing to do but get reckless and chuckle over the naughty baby. I went the limit. The bucket-shop crashed on Roger's head. He tried to pull up, chucked his money in, and other people's, but it wouldn't save it. Clear case of dirty work. A greasy bubble, Cascan Oil. Left a nasty mess when it burst. And all the papers signed in Roger's name.

Telephone rang in the next room while we were in here. I was sitting where you are, Trevor. Roger looks at me with a kind of crooked smile. 'Come with me,' he says, and I went. Into that room, the library. Roger didn't trouble to switch on the light; the telephone was on the desk beside the door. The police were after him, said the man on the telephone—the police after Sir Roger Poole, Bart., M.P., and all the rest of it! 'Listen,' says Roger. And I listened while he told me a few things about myself. 'A poor husk of a man,' he called me. 'A graveyard of a brother you are,' he said. 'And the epitaph on your grave will be *Dolor Ira*,' he said, for Roger was a great Latin scholar and could lash out bits of Tacitus as easily as a parson might give you the Bible. I thought he was going to shoot me, I was ready for it—but he'd shot himself. Roger loved me, you know—"

"Then why the hell," Tarlyon blazed out, "did you take this cursed house?"

Antony mauled his cigar.

"Because," he said with a grin, "it just happened that way. It was fate to find it empty—a fine, large house like this at a low rent while all England was yelling for houses. But I might not have taken it if Diavalen had been against it—"

"Oh," said Tarlyon to that.

Antony looked at his wrist-watch, and jumped up in a mighty hurry. "God, the time's gone! Excuse me a moment."

"We will not!" cried Tarlyon, and had his back against the library door almost before you saw him leave the table.

But Antony walked his way to the library door without a word.

"Don't, old Antony, don't!" Tarlyon begged.

"Out of my way!" said Antony. He said it as though he was thinking of something else, which was Antony's most dangerous way of saying anything.

Now Red Antony was a giant, and irresponsible at that. The two of us couldn't have held him from that library door.

Tarlyon let him pass with a wicked word, and has regretted it ever since. Antony slammed the door behind him, and we heard the twist of the key.

Without a word to me Tarlyon was at the French window; opened it, and disappeared. I stayed. I was extremely uncomfortable in that mad-house, you understand. Perhaps two minutes passed, perhaps ten. Where the devil was Tarlyon? And then I heard through the library door the thud of something falling. And then in there a window smashed, a sharp smash. I measured my distance from that door and crashed my shoulder at it, and fell into the library on top of the panel.

"Light," said Tarlyon's voice. I switched it on. On the floor between us was a heap of a man face downwards, with the back of a red head half-screwed under an outstretched arm. And there was red on the back of Tarlyon's hand where he had put it through the window.

We knelt each side of Red Antony, and turned him over.

"Dead," I said.

"Not he!" said Tarlyon. "He's fainted—from fright." But he knew as well as I did that Antony was dead—from fright. The huge bulk was as limp as a half-filled sack as we lifted it a little. Antony's eyes were wide open, and they were like the eyes of a child that has just been thrashed.

"He's been shot," I said suddenly.

"There was no noise," said Tarlyon, but he looked at me. There had been no noise, but there was the faint, acrid taste of pistol-smoke in the air. It's unmistakable, that faint, acrid smell of a revolver just spent. But Antony had not been shot.

"It wasn't an illusion, then!" Tarlyon whispered softly. "That smell . . . of Roger's revolver! And it's killed Antony in the end!"

I stared down at the poor haunted face. And then I heard Tarlyon whisper: "My God!" And again: "My God—look at that!" But I did not look. I knew he was staring over my shoulder, and I was afraid to look. I was afraid of what I would see. And then I twisted my head over my shoulder, towards the far end of the room, where there was a little door from the hall. And I saw the thing sitting squat in the corner, the black thing with white teeth flashing in a white face and a gardenia in her hair. In the palm of one hand was a little golden bowl, and from this bowl floated up a wisp of smoke, just a wisp of smoke against the blackness of her dress, and this was the faint, acrid smell of a spent bullet. And Diavalen was laughing—the dumb woman was laughing with all the glory of ivory teeth and scarlet lips. . . . We left the thing to its joke. We went out by the window, and did not remember our hats and sticks.

# The Real Reason why Shelmerdene was Late for Dinner

"Lord Tarlyon on the telephone, madam."

"I cannot speak to him, Foster. You can see very well that I cannot speak to him and why I cannot speak to him, and so why didn't you ask him his message straight away? And take away that towel and bring another not so new. You know very well, Foster, that one cannot dry oneself properly with a new towel. And then ask Lord Tarlyon what he has to say for himself?"

Foster returned.

"His lordship is sorry he disturbed you, madam, and rang up merely to beg you to be punctual for dinner at half-past eight. And may he send his car for you?"

"Tell his lordship," said Shelmerdene, "that I am always punctual. Add, Foster, that punctuality is the only servile quality I have. And he may send his car for me. Thank him. And for Heaven's sake, Foster, close those drawers! You know I can't bear open drawers in a room. I knew something was worrying me."

In the fullness of time Shelmerdene emerged from her bath and re-entered her bedroom. Her dressing-gown was of white velvet trimmed with ermine and lined with jade green charmeuse. She sat at the toilet-table and looked at herself in the mirror.

"Foster!" called Shelmerdene, softly, vaguely.

"Yes, madam?"

"What shall I wear to-night?"

"Well, madam. . . ."

"Oh, dear! why are English maids so stupid! Why have they no taste! Why must good maids always be French? Oh, Foster, what shall I do? You are so lacking in ideas, in *finesse*, in judgment, in all sartorial courtliness! On the other hand, you are a very nice girl and I like you very much, and, anyway, you are clean, which is a good deal more than some of my friends are, what with being in a hurry and powder being so cheap. I withdraw everything I said previous to that last sentence, Foster."

"There is the black sequin, madam. . . ."

"There is certainly the black sequin, Foster. And there has been the black sequin ever since the Armistice. You may have it for yourself, Foster, for being such an ass."

"Oh, thank you, madam!"

"So you say, but what will really happen will be that you will wear that black sequin dress one night at the Hammersmith Palais de Danse, which I hear is very modish these days, and some young man will take a fancy to you, and you will marry him, and then where will I be? I ask you, Foster, where will I be?"

"Oh, but, madam, I would never, never leave you!"

"Pouf!" said Shelmerdene. "But, talking of that, Foster, how would you like it if I married again? Or if my husband came back? Ah, yes," said Shelmerdene softly, "if he came back. . . ."

Foster did not know what to say. She wanted to ask a few questions. She was a nice girl, but she wanted frightfully to ask a few questions. She whispered:

"Do you think, madam, he will?"

Shelmerdene looked at her for a long, long time. Shelmerdene's eyes were blue, they were as blue as night.

"I don't know, Foster. He has been gone a very long time, you know—ten years is a long time, isn't it? He was a very grim sort of man, let me tell you, and he made a very great mistake. And I was very young, and I made a great mistake. So there you are, Foster. Silly, isn't it?"

And Shelmerdene looked at Foster for a long, long time; but Foster was quite sure that her mistress did not see her. She waited. . . .

"You see, Foster, life is an awful mess, and men are extraordinary. You will notice, when you meet your young man at the Palais de Danse, how very extraordinary men are. They are always jealous about the wrong things . . . and now I am thirty-four years old! I am thirty-four years old, Foster! Oh, dear, it is perfectly amazing how soon one becomes thirty-four years old!"

And Foster whispered:

"And did he go away, madam—just like that?"

"Don't whisper, girl! We are speaking of commonplace things—love—never whisper about love, Foster! All the trouble in the world has come from whispering about love. I saw him going— day by day, night by night, I saw him going, and I let him go. I was too proud, too proud. But I am not proud now. You will, of course, bear me out in that?"

"Well, madam, I think you've got a great sort of pride—the sort, madam, that lets you let your friends use you as much as they like while you sit down and despise them all by yourself. I've watched you often, if I may say so, madam."

"Muddled but pleasant, Foster. But if you had listened to what I was saying instead of thinking out how best you could slander those of my friends you like least, you would have realised I was talking about pride, not dignity. There is too much muck in pride, Foster. Remember that in your wretched moments. But I was very proud then, and I let him go, that queer, grim, good-looking man. He was very good-looking, Foster, in a naval sort of way—but what a fool! Oh, my God, what a fool!"

And Foster whispered:

"And if he came back now, madam—would you. . . .?"

"Ah," said Shelmerdene, "you ask me what I don't know. Ten years is a very long time, as I remarked before. I am in the fourth decade of my life, Foster, and I must have understanding. I know too much about love to want only love. Love, Foster, is just a trick of the heart to fool the mind—without understanding, it is no use to me. It is funny how well Englishmen can understand

niggers and how idiotic they can be about women. They get so
sleepy, Foster. . . . If he came back now, would I let him? I don't
know, I can't tell. If he came back sweetly—oh, sweetly, Foster!
then yes, yes, yes! But if he came back bitterly. . . . I will wear the
new silver tissue from Lanvin, Foster. And the silver shoes—
there, in that box from Hellstern. I am thirty-four years old, and
I would like to look—"

"Here it is, madam. It *is* a lovely dress!"

"Yes, it will do very well. I shall look like a greyhound to-
night, though of course there will be no man there to notice it.
I have often looked like a greyhound, but there is only one man
who has ever remarked it. A very inadequate crowd of men
about, Foster. If I could only write a book I would write one
on men, and I would call it *Rats, Rape and Rheumatism*. Oh,
what fun I would have with that book, Foster! Imagine the face
of a publisher when I took him a book with that title! He would
say: 'Eh—but—eh—we cannot publish a book like this, you
know!' And I would say: 'And why not, pray? Look at Mrs.
Asquith.' And after we had looked at Mrs. Asquith he would
publish my book at once, and then I would go into Hatchard's
in Piccadilly and ask Mr. Humphreys: 'And how is my book
going, Mr. Humphreys?' 'I beg your pardon?' he would say.
'Yes, Mr. Humphreys, my book, *Rats, Rape and Rheumatism*.'
And I would say that very loud, you see, Foster, and every one in
the shop would look at me, whispering among themselves:
'There is that terrible woman who wrote that terrible book!'
And with one accord, in fact one might almost say in a body,
they would drop the trash they had thought of buying and buy
my book, for it is not every day, Foster, that a woman writes a
book called *Rats, Rape and Rheumatism*."

"I am sure you could write a very good book, madam. Your
life would make such an interesting novel!"

"Oh, every woman thinks that! It is extraordinary how
conceited women are about their past miseries. I can bear

women less and less. And oh, I wish I was not going out to dinner tonight! I would like to dine on an egg and then read a good book. What are you reading, Foster?"

"Well, madam. . . . It's by Ethel M. Dell."

"Is it any good? I have never read any of Miss Dell's books. But then I have never read any of Henry James's either, not right through."

"Well, madam . . . It's a love-story, about a girl and an earl, you know."

"No, Foster, I don't know. There are earls and earls, and, if you will forgive me, some need belting and some don't. Will you bring the book and read it out to me? Please, Foster. You haven't read out to me for such a long time."

"Well, madam, here it is. Chapter One.

" 'I shall go to sea to-morrow,' said Saltash, with sudden decision. 'I'm so tired of this place, Larpent—fed up to repletion.'

" 'Then by all means let us go, my lord!' said Larpent, with the faint glimmer of a smile behind his beard, which was the only expression of humour he ever permitted himself.' "

"Give me the nail-file, Foster."

" 'Saltash turned and surveyed the sky-line over the yacht's rail with obvious discontent on his ugly face. His eyes were odd, one black, one gray, giving a curiously unstable appearance to a countenance which otherwise might have claimed to possess some strength. His brows were black and deeply marked—' "

"Foster, have you taken that stain off the blue serge?"

"Yes, madam. 'A certain arrogance, a certain royalty of bearing characterised him. Whatever he did—and his actions were often far from praiseworthy—this careless distinction of mien always marked him. He received an almost involuntary respect wherever he went—' "

"Thank you, Foster. That is very nice. I don't wonder this Saltash man received an almost involuntary respect wherever he went, what with having one gray eye and one black one. I once met a man with a black eye, but I don't think I've ever met a man with eyes of various colours, earl or commoner. But perhaps I will meet one to-night, Foster, and fall in love with him! Oh, dear, it *is* such a long time since I was in love with any one! What shall I do, Foster?"

"You had better let me do your hair now, madam. It's getting on."

"Yes, but how awful it would be never never to fall in love again! Particularly now that the days are drawing in. Don't pull so hard, Foster. Hair is, after all, but hair. Wintering in England is a cold business without a man in one's life. There's that wretched telephone again! You're hurting me, girl! If it's Mrs. Loyalty tell her I can't lunch with her to-morrow, after all. I shall not be well tomorrow, I feel."

Foster went to the telephone on the little table by the bed.

"Hallo! Hallo! Is that Mayfair 2794?"

"Yes," said Foster. "Who is that speaking, please?"

"Is that Mrs.—?" asked the voice.

"Who is that speaking, please?"

"I say," said the voice, "just tell Mrs.—that I would like to speak to her, would you?"

"I'm afraid, sir, that madam will not speak to you unless you give your name."

"What's your name?" asked the voice.

"Foster, sir."

"Well, look here, Foster, don't be an ass all your life, be a dear instead and just ask your mistress to come to the telephone. It's most important, tell her—"

Shelmerdene said, icily, from her chair:

"I hope, Foster, that you are having an entertaining conversation. May I ask how it concerns me?"

"Gentleman wants to speak to you, madam. Gives no name."

"Any remarks?"

"He has a very pleasant voice, madam."

Shelmerdene went to the telephone. She sat on the edge of the bed.

"Hallo, hallo!" said the voice.

"Just a moment," said Shelmerdene. Her dressing-gown had slipped off her knee and her knee was cold, so she rearranged the dressing-gown over her knee.

SHELMERDENE: Now!

THE VOICE: At last, Shelmerdene! How are you, dear?

SHELMERDENE: I am very well, thank you. May I know to whom I am giving this information?

THE VOICE: Shelmerdene! Do you really mean to say that you don't recognise my voice?

SHELMERDENE: I am sorry. I do hate to hurt people. And you have a very nice voice, too!

THE VOICE: Thank you, Shelmerdene. (*Bitterly*) Well, as you don't recognise my voice I had better go away. Are you sure you don't, my dear?

SHELMERDENE: Well, you know, the profusion of endearing epithets in your conversation leads me to conclude that you are either a friend or a person of colossal cheek. But now I come to think of it, I have a vague idea about you. You have the voice of a man I dined with once.

THE VOICE: Ah yes! You dined with me once—upon a time.

SHELMERDENE: Oh, *la, la!* I said *once*, my friend.

THE VOICE: You were never a great mathematician, Shelmerdene. But what does it matter how often we dined, so long as we did dine? And ever since then I have remem-bered you, for there are very few beautiful women, even in one's dreams. Therefore I have rung you up, after all these years.

SHELMERDENE: Thank you, stranger. You speak very prettily. Are you trying to pretend that you were in love with me at that distant time?

THE VOICE: I think I am in love with you now.

SHELMERDENE: You *think*! You are not very dexterous, sir. . . .

THE VOICE: You are sitting on the edge of the bed now. Please, no ceremony with me, Shelmerdene! Lie down on the bed, dear—you will be more comfortable so, on that virginal bed!

SHELMERDENE: Irony, my friend, does not become the moment. It is a vulgarity peculiar to cultured men. It is a knack, and I don't like knacks. Shall I ring off?

THE VOICE: No, no! Please!

SHELMERDENE: Well, a moment. (*To Foster*) Leave us, Foster.

THE VOICE: Shelmerdene, you are very hard!

SHELMERDENE: No, I am very tired . . . of hardness. You understand?

THE VOICE: I want to hear about your life, Shelmerdene. I have not seen you for so long! Do things still happen to you, and do you still let them happen?

SHELMERDENE: How bitter you are, aren't you, in a hidden sort of way!

THE VOICE: Do things still happen to you, Shelmerdene?

SHELMERDENE: No.

THE VOICE: So abrupt!

SHELMERDENE: I was thinking of your voice, I like it, but it's bitter.

THE VOICE: I have drunk vinegar.

SHELMERDENE: But I thought they called it gin-and-bitters in the navy!

THE VOICE: Have it your own way, Shelmerdene. But you have still told me nothing of yourself.

SHELMERDENE: But what am I to tell you? What is the use of my telling you that I have been in love only once in my life? You will not believe me. . . . But it is true, you know. Though, of course, there was a time when I was inquisitive.

THE VOICE: And that has passed?

SHELMERDENE: That has passed.

THE VOICE: But isn't life very dull for you, then? What do you do?

SHELMERDENE: I wait.

THE VOICE: So serious!

SHELMERDENE: I must go on with my dressing now. I am very late.

THE VOICE: A moment, please, please! You said you had been in love only once in your life. Tell me of that.

SHELMERDENE: But the man's mad! What is there to tell? It ended—it just ended! He said, you know, that love was like religion, for it must be done well or not at all. . . . And that's all there is of it. He went. One can't explain an ideal, one can only explain the failure of an ideal. One can't describe a love-affair, one can only describe the end of a love-affair. I loved him, I lost him. And I'm still alive—and so, I suppose, is he! I wonder if he is a little softer than he was. . . .

THE VOICE: And so you ended a beautiful thing because of a caprice?

SHELMERDENE: Oh, for God's sake don't use that horrible word—"caprice!" It is just a label given to women by half-witted men. It is the name disappointed men give to women's constancy. No, no, never use that silly word again! Besides, it is not worthy of your pleasant voice.

THE VOICE: Bother my voice! And how, why, did your one real love-affair end?

SHELMERDENE: We were too proud, you see. I was very young, and he would not understand. He simply would not understand!

THE VOICE: (*Impatiently*) But what is it that he would not understand? Women are always complaining of that. . . .

SHELMERDENE: *Please* don't generalise! It is so easy to insult a woman by saying women. How did he fail? Oh, he would not understand that marriage is comradeship, not domination. It is very difficult for some men to understand that, and it is very difficult for some women to be dominated.

THE VOICE: It is very difficult for some women to be loyal!

SHELMERDENE: Again! Well, perhaps. Loyalty, like a sense of humour, is a quality universally praised because everyone thinks he or she has it. And when you say that a woman is lacking in loyalty you really mean that she is not so celibate as you might wish. When you say that it is difficult for some women to be loyal, what you really mean is that it is difficult for some women to be celibate. You are quite right, it is. And why, in God's name, should they be? Must all Englishwomen be made of stone because most Englishmen are educated only from the throat downwards! Now, tell me why did you ring me up—was it to discuss, "loyalty"?

THE VOICE: Your voice hurts rather, Shelmerdene. I have just returned to England.

SHELMERDENE: (*Very softly*) Yes?

THE VOICE: I was very ill, in Ceylon. And then one night, when I was better, I was wandering about the veranda of my friend's station, and I happened to hear the whirr of the P. and O. from Colombo to England. It was very distant, four miles away at least, but the night was very, very still, and I not only heard the whirr but above it a twitter—a tinkling something—a very faint, long-drawn silly something, which could only be the music of the liner's orchestra—

SHELMERDENE: Yes? I am listening.

THE VOICE: That is what I heard, Shelmerdene, and it somehow made me see things very far away. I who had been abroad so long, saw England. Funny, wasn't it? And I saw *you*—I saw you dancing, Shelmerdene! I saw you dancing as I last saw you, dancing very gaily and subtly through the maze of the Avalons' ballroom, and smiling up into your partner's face. How well you danced, Shelmerdene! Do you still dance so well?

SHELMERDENE: Dancing changes.

THE VOICE: Of course. And men and women die.

SHELMERDENE: But dancing is the only thing that changes.

THE VOICE: But I was telling you of my vision, that night in Ceylon. And in my vision, you somehow looked like a greyhound—Hallo, hallo! What is it?

SHELMERDENE: Nothing, nothing! Go on.

THE VOICE: But there is no more, Shelmerdene! I came home. Now tell me a little about yourself—about the only man you've ever really loved! Did you say he was your husband?

SHELMERDENE: He *is* my husband.

THE VOICE: Really! In spite of everything, you mean? Now, tell me, Shelmerdene—

SHELMERDENE: You mock. I will not tell you anything, because you mock. Yes, you are hard, and you mock. I made a mistake when I said that you had the voice of a man I dined with once. You have the voice of a man who has played with many women—

THE VOICE: Simply because I loved one unhappily! And you, Shelmerdene—and *you!* Why, I can see the whole procession of your past, the long procession of the men who have loved you, the men you have touched! Oh, my God!

SHELMERDENE: Silence, silence, silence! What I have done I have done because I wanted the world, but you have done it because you wanted revenge. What I have done I have done because I have too much heart, but you have done it because you have no heart. Through the telephone I can hear that you have no heart, and I can see the hole where your heart should be. My life has made me sad, but yours has made you bitter—oh, why, why?

THE VOICE: Heavens, how do I know! I am as God made me—

SHELMERDENE: No, no! You are much worse!

THE VOICE: Then I am as you made me.

SHELMERDENE: That is why my eyes are wet.

THE VOICE: Come, come, Shelmerdene, don't be silly! We ran amok, that's all—

SHELMERDENE: That's all! I did not think I would live to see my own tragedy fulfilled—but I see it fulfilled in you! Isn't that strange?

THE VOICE: All this, my dear, is quite beyond me. Will you answer a simple question? Suppose your husband—who you say was the only man you have ever loved and who, I am certain, has never loved any other woman but you—suppose this husband of yours came back to England and rang you up—to ask you to dine with him?

SHELMERDENE: Just because, after all these years, he suddenly remembered her one night! Just because, after all these years, he suddenly saw a vision of her dancing—as he had last seen her, he who had suddenly, bitterly, vengefully, left her life because, being a child, she had taken a silly fancy to make him jealous! Oh, no, no! I would not dine with him—like that. Life is not like that. I do not know what life is like, for I am not yet a million years old, but I know that it is not like that. It is not so easy as that.

THE VOICE: My God, how efficiently you damn him, don't you! That would be your answer? . . . Hallo, hallo! Would that be your answer, Shelmerdene, if he came back like—me—

SHELMERDENE: Just like you?

THE VOICE: Well?

SHELMERDENE: He would just be a man I had dined with once.

*(A Silence.)*

THE VOICE: I am sorry to have disturbed you. Good-night.

SHELMERDENE: Come back again, but—

THE VOICE: Good-night, Shelmerdene.

SHELMERDENE:—but sweetly, Gerald! Oh, my dear, sweetly!

THE VOICE: (*Very faintly*) Good-bye, Shelmerdene.

*(There is a soft click at the other end.)*

SHELMERDENE: Good-bye, you ass!

Then Foster came in, with an anxious face.

"The car is here, madam."

Shelmerdene turned to her.

"Gracious, madam, however will you go out with your eyes like that? Oh, dear!"

"Hurry, Foster; dress me! I shall be terribly late!"

The End of These Charming People.

## The Green Hat

**Michael Arlen**. *Introduced by Kirsty Gunn*
*The Green Hat* perfectly reflects the atmosphere of the 1920s – the post-war fashion for verbal smartness, youthful cynicism and the spirit of rebellion of the 'bright young things' of Mayfair.

## The Incredulity of Father Brown

**GK Chesterton**. *Introduced by Ann Widdecombe*
Sensation followed the sudden death of Chesterton's eccentric sleuth; as well it might, when he sat up in his coffin and applied a little quiet detachment to the incident. But then sensation was implicit in all the cases Father Brown so modestly handled.

## The Unbearable Bassington

**Saki**. *Introduced by Evelyn Waugh*
A biting satire on the conceits of high society and an exquisite novel of manners, *The Unbearable Bassington* is also an incisive piece of writing, anticipating the early works of Evelyn Waugh, whose introduction to an earlier edition is included in this edition. Here is Edwardian society on Saki's inimitable skewer.

## Gryll Grange

**Thomas Love Peacock**. *Introduced by Anthony Lejeune*
Peacock's position in English literature is unique. There was nothing like his style of novel before his time; unless it might have occurred to Jonathan Swift to invent a story as a vehicle for the dialogue of his *Polite Conversation*. A kindly satire on the mid-Victorian age, *Gryll Grange* is considered by many to be Peacock's late life masterpiece.

**www.capuchin-classics.co.uk**